DISARMING HIS HEART

ALSO BY WINNIE GRIGGS

Historical Romance

Talulla Sawyer

The Unexpected Bride

Her Tailor-Made Husband

His Christmas Matchmaker

The Hope's Haven Amish Romance Series

Her Amish Wedding Quilt (Book 1)

Her Amish Springtime Miracle (Book 2)

Her Amish Patchwork Family (Book 3)

Other Books

Once Upon A Texas Christmas

Her Tailor-Made Husband

Texas Cinderella

A Matter Of Trust

His Christmas Matchmaker

Second Chance Hero

Lone Star Heiress

A Family For Christmas

The Bride Next Door

Handpicked Husband

A Baby Between Them

Second Chance Family

The Proper Wife

The Christmas Journey

The Hand-Me-Down Family

A Will of Her Own

Something More

Novellas

The Road Home

Home For Thanksgiving

A complete list of titles by Winnie can be found on her website at https://www.winniegriggs.com/booklist.html

DISARMING HIS
Heart

BY

WINNIE GRIGGS

the Pink
Pistol
SISTERHOOD

BOOK 6

Excerpt from:
One Shot at Love (Pink Pistol Sisterhood Series) by Linda Broday
Copyright (c) 2023 Linda Broday

Cover Artist Kim Killion of The Killion Group

Editor Annie Sarac at Victory Editing

Published by WinOver LLC

ISBN 978-1-949423-11-2

Version 2023.05

To Chris who helped me in any number of ways, from brainstorming, to helping me push through writer's block to just giving me a kick in the pants when I needed one. You've been on this writer's journey with me from the beginning and your support and friendship has meant the world to me.

1

Larkin, Missouri, May 1911

Violet Taylor sat in the storeroom of Adeline's Fashion Emporium, trying not to bite the fingernails on her good hand. It was a bad habit, one she'd worked hard to overcome.

But when she was really anxious, like now, the urge came creeping back. Violet shifted, adjusting the fit of the sling she wore around her neck. She heard the murmur of voices on the other side of the storeroom door. But neither voice was Lily's. One of the voices was Adeline's, and the other must have been a customer's.

After seven months it was still hard to think of the dress-shop owner as Aunt Adeline. The seamstress was more Lily's aunt than hers. Since she and Lily were twins, it meant Adeline Clemmons was related to her as well.

The ringing of the shop bell alerted her that the street door had opened. Was someone leaving or entering? A moment later she heard the unmistakable sound of Lily's breezy voice greeting her aunt. Violet's stomach fluttered and she stood, no longer able to sit still. No matter how much Wyatt said this plan of his was going to work, she still wasn't sure asking Lily to do this for her was the right thing.

A few minutes later her sister entered the storeroom.

And halted on the threshold.

"Violet! Oh goodness, you're hurt." Lily quickly closed the door behind her. "What happened and how bad is it?"

Violet envied the presence her sister had. The two of them might be identical twins, but Lily merely had to enter a room to instantly draw all eyes to her—and it was all the more remarkable because she seemed completely unaware she had that effect. Violet, on the other hand, knew herself to be a wallflower, easily overlooked and dismissed.

But Lily was still studying her in some concern, so Violet brought her thoughts back to the current situation and lifted her right elbow, sling and all. "It's not serious, just a sprain. But it's actually the reason we're here."

Before she finished talking, the back door opened and Wyatt stepped inside to join them. Wyatt Gleason had been a part of Violet's life for almost as long as she could remember. He was her best friend and her confidant. They looked after each other—in short, he was like a big brother to her.

But Lily cast him an accusatory glance. "You didn't tell me she was hurt."

He shrugged and crossed his arms. "I thought it best to save all explanations until we could speak freely."

Violet didn't understand the friction that crackled between Wyatt and Lily on the few occasions they'd been together. Somehow, the two of them had gotten off on the wrong foot from the very beginning. Which didn't make sense as it was Wyatt who'd managed to track down Lily and Aunt Adeline and reunite the three of them seven months ago.

But now was not the time to ponder that, so she quickly grabbed the conversational reins. "I sprained my wrist two days ago." She took her seat again. "Doc said if I ever want to shoot with any degree of accuracy in the future that I have to wear this sling for at least four weeks." Which was a serious consideration since she made her living performing as a sharpshooter with a traveling show.

Lily finished crossing the room and touched Violet's uninjured arm. "I'm so sorry. Regardless of what you said, this does sound serious. But it's not the end of the world. If you do like the doctor said, the Masked Marvel will be awing the crowds with her skill again in no time."

The Masked Marvel was the name Violet used when she performed her sharpshooter routine. It came from the fact that she wore a mask and costume to keep her identity secret.

Violet grimaced and slid over on the bench to make room for her sister. "I agree. But it's not quite that simple."

Lily arranged her skirts as she sat. "Why not?"

"The Masked Marvel is a big draw for the circus." She usually spoke of her circus-act identity in the third person. "She needs to make an appearance whether she performs her act or not. She'll ride in the opening parade and maybe walk through the crowds a time or two."

Lily didn't seem convinced. "So you just add the sling to your costume for the next month." She waved a hand airily. "It'll just make you seem all the more dangerous and mysterious."

Surely that wasn't a touch of envy in Lily's voice? "But if the Masked Marvel and Violet Taylor both appear with slings at the same time, it won't take long for people to start figuring out they're the same person."

"Oh. I see." Lily's expression took on a thoughtful cast. Then she smiled brightly. "Well then, you get someone to pretend to be the Masked Marvel without the sling."

It was Wyatt who answered this time. "Good idea. But it won't work for two reasons. One, the accident happened while she was in costume, so lots of people know the Masked Marvel was injured. And two, even if that wasn't the case, if the Masked Marvel isn't injured, then whoever is wearing the costume would be expected to shoot. And no one can shoot like Vi."

Lily grimaced. "I'm sorry. You've obviously already thought this out before you came here." She turned back to Violet. "You said you need my help. What can I do?"

Violet shared a look with Wyatt, wondering how to ask such a big favor of the sister she'd only reconnected with seven months ago. For a moment neither of them spoke.

In the meantime, the storeroom door opened again and Aunt Adeline walked in, leaving the door slightly ajar behind her. "Mrs. Givens finally left, and I put a GONE TO LUNCH sign on the door so we can have some privacy." She looked from one to the other. "So what did I miss?"

Adeline Clemmons was a petite, white-haired woman with a charming smile and grandmotherly demeanor. But Violet could sense an unexpected inner strength and determination in her. Based on her appearance, she could be any age from forty-five to sixty-five. And though Lily called her Aunt Adeline, she was really their great-aunt, the sister of their grandmother.

It was Lily who answered her question. "You haven't missed much. Violet and Wyatt were just about to ask me a favor." She turned to Violet with an impatient toss of her head. "Oh, for goodness' sake. Whatever it is, just ask."

Violet stood and gave Aunt Adeline her seat. Then she took a deep breath, locked gazes with Lily, and blurted out her request. "I want you to swap places with me."

Lily sat up straighter. "What?"

The older woman put a gentle hand on Lily's skirt.

But Violet kept her gaze locked on her twin. It was so important that she make Lily understand. "I know it's a lot to ask, but it would only be for a few weeks." Violet waved with her good hand. "It's the perfect solution, the only solution really. You can wear the sling when you're in costume so no one will expect you to do any shooting. And when you're being just plain old Violet, you can use your arm freely. It'll also have the added benefit of completely throwing off any suspicions."

"I'd like to help, but I can't just drop everything and head off to whatever town your circus is parked in. I have responsibilities here." She gestured toward their aunt. "I can't ask Aunt Adeline to run this place by herself."

But their aunt blithely waved off that concern. "Don't let me hold you back. I can keep the shop running on my own if it's just for a few weeks."

Violet shot a quick, grateful look her aunt's way, then turned back to Lily. "She wouldn't have to. While you're pretending to be me, I'll be right here pretending to be you." She grimaced self-consciously. "I know I don't have your fashion expertise, but I can help in other ways." She cast a rather shy glance at the lady sitting beside Lily. "And it'll give me a chance to get to know Aunt Adeline a bit better."

Her aunt's expression softened. "I'd like that as well, my dear. We've lost so many years."

That seemed to give Lily pause. "If I agree to do this," she said slowly, then held up a hand. "And I'm not yet convinced I should. But if I do, what would I need to do?"

Some of the tension eased from Violet's shoulders. She hadn't been at all certain Lily would agree to the plan, but at least she seemed willing to consider it. "Nothing too difficult. You would wear the Masked Marvel costume to make an appearance in any parades when the circus arrives in a new town and at the opening of the show. But my act won't be performed until my arm is healed, so you won't have to handle any firearms."

Some of Lily's own tension seemed to ease. "Good."

While Violet was an expert marksman, it was no secret that Lily absolutely refused to have anything to do with guns. Not due to any moral or societal constraints but because they terrified her.

"And what about when I'm not in costume?"

"I have some other minor duties with the circus that you'll be expected to take care of. Wyatt can make sure you know all the wheres, whens and hows. Otherwise, your time is your own. And you would live in my wagon. It's not very large, but it's comfortable and private."

Lily nodded, then turned to her aunt. "What about you? Do you truly think you can manage the shop on your own for a month?" She glanced her sister's way. "No offense, but I don't think you know much about fabrics and trims, not to mention taking measurements and making alterations."

Aunt Adeline jumped in before Violet could respond. "We'll be just fine. I'm sure Violet is a quick study. Besides, many of our customers know just what they want, so it's only a matter of taking their orders. And she'll have her sling as an excuse not to actually do fittings or take measurements or anything else physical."

Lily turned to Wyatt. "What about you? Do you think we can succeed at fooling everyone?" Her tone and expression held a note of challenge.

He spread his hands. "Since this was my idea in the first place, I'd say I'm solidly behind the plan."

She stared at him a moment longer, then nodded. "Where is the circus right now?"

"On the way to East Texas. We'll be touring several towns there over the next few months."

Lily gave a mock pout. "I suppose it was too much to

expect someplace exciting like New Orleans or New York." Then she turned serious again and met Violet's gaze. "How soon would this swap need to take place?"

"The sooner the better. Wyatt has train tickets in hand for tomorrow."

"And just how long is *a few weeks*?"

Violet cupped her right elbow with her left hand. "Doc said it would probably take about four weeks for my arm to heal properly."

"Oh." Lily managed to infuse a wealth of disappointment in that one syllable. Did that mean she *wasn't* going to agree to their plan?

"What is it?"

Lily traced a circle on the bench with her finger. "I've been working with Pastor Carson on a children's program for the church's twenty-fifth anniversary celebration. The performance is scheduled for the twenty-third."

Violet's heart fell. That was just three weeks away. And she knew Lily had formed an attachment to the town's pastor. There was no way she'd want to miss such a big event.

She was just about to tell her sister she understood and would find another way to tackle her problem when Lily straightened.

She gave Violet a determined look. "So you'll not only need to take my place leading the practice sessions but you'll also have to direct the actual performance." Then she grinned. "But you're used to performing in front of crowds, so perhaps you'll do a better job of it than I have. I have to admit there was a bit more to directing the children than I'd expected."

Violet wasn't particularly excited about taking over that aspect of Lily's life, but she was too relieved to worry about that at the moment. "Does that mean you'll do it?"

Her sister nodded. "Of course. I know how much keeping

your Masked Marvel identity a secret is to you. And I know you'd do the same for me."

"I absolutely would. Oh Lily, you're so generous to disrupt your life to help me this way."

Lily grinned. "To be honest, a part of me is actually looking forward to it. I've barely been outside of Larkin since I moved here as a little girl." She waved a hand. "But you get to travel freely around the country. And you receive admiration and accolades almost nightly from the audiences you perform for."

Violet grimaced. "It's not nearly as glamorous as you make it sound."

Her sister was undeterred. "I guess I'm about to find that out." Then her eyes narrowed slightly as she shot Violet a stern look. "Just make sure you don't let the pastor down—everything has to go perfectly."

"You have my word." Violet gave Lily's hand a squeeze. "I know how much he means to you."

They shared a meaningful glance, which was interrupted when Wyatt cleared his throat.

"Now that that's settled, we need to lay out a plan."

Lily wrinkled her nose. "What kind of plan?"

"Like Violet said, you and I will board the train headed to Jefferson, Texas, tomorrow to meet up with the circus. I can fill you in during the trip on most of what you need to know about living Violet's life. And I'm certain your Aunt Adeline can do the same for Violet. But I figured you ladies would want to spend what time you have left today to answer any questions you might have of a more personal nature, things that are likely to come up when you're pretending to be the other."

The sound of someone knocking on the shop door interrupted their conversation.

Aunt Adeline popped up from her seat. "Oh dear, I forgot

Edda Rodgers had a twelve-thirty appointment for a fitting." She placed a hand on Lily's shoulder as she started to get up. "You stay right here. I'll take care of her. Or better yet, why don't you take Violet and Wyatt to our quarters upstairs where you'll all be more comfortable. Just give me a few minutes to get Edda into the fitting room." And with that the dressmaker bustled out, carefully closing the door behind her.

As Lily stood, she glanced from Violet to Wyatt and back again. "You two have obviously had more time to think this through than I have. What do you see as the obstacles we'll have to overcome? Other than the obvious, of course."

Wyatt raised a brow. "The obvious?"

"Yes. I won't know any of the people in Violet's world, and she won't know any of the folks in mine. There are bound to be references in conversations that we don't understand."

Violet nodded. "Yes, well, we're hoping that you'll stay close to Wyatt and I'll stay close to Aunt Adeline so they can help smooth over any of those awkward moments."

"Is there anyone we'll want to let in on our secret?"

"Just a handful. We figured for this to work, it would be best to keep the circle as small as possible. Why? Do you feel differently?"

"I'm thinking we'll want to let Dr. Matthews know."

Violet frowned. "Why? I don't expect the arm to give me any trouble."

"You can't be certain of that. But there's another reason. If you walk around town wearing that sling, he'll wonder why he wasn't involved in putting it there."

"Oh, that makes sense. Can the good doctor be trusted to keep our secret?"

"He's very discreet." Then Lily's lips curved in a mischievous grin. "Besides, he's a widower and I think he's a bit smitten with Aunt Adeline."

Violet filed that little nugget of insight away as she

returned Lily's smile. "Is there anyone else you think will notice anything amiss?"

Her sister pondered that for a moment, then finally shook her head. "You wouldn't be able to fool Gertie of course—she's my best friend and knows me almost better than I know myself. But fortunately she's out of town, visiting her sister in St. Louis."

"But will she be gone for the full four weeks?"

"Oh, good question. She's due back the day before the celebration." Lily waved a hand. "But if it becomes necessary to tell her, you can do so with the assurance that she's entirely trustworthy." She straightened. "I think we've given Aunt Adeline enough time. Follow me and I'll escort you upstairs."

Later, after Violet and her sister had exhausted their exchange of information, Violet volunteered to help Lily decide what to pack.

"You won't need to bring much," Violet warned. "To make our swap believable, you'll need to wear my things." She fingered some of the gowns hanging in Lily's wardrobe. "And I'm sorry, but my dresses aren't even close to being as lovely and elegant as yours." Would she be able to wear such finery with the same confidence and poise as Lily?

Lily gave Violet an assessing look. "There's nothing wrong with the way you dress. Of course, if you wanted to show a little more dash, you'd just need to add a bit of the right kind of trim, adjust a neckline or hemline. But even that is just a small part of it. Real flair comes from the way you carry yourself regardless of what you're wearing."

Easier said than done. Violet grabbed her carpet bag and started unpacking so she didn't have to meet her sister's gaze. "I'll try to do you proud while you're away."

Lily rushed over and gave her a hug. "That wasn't what I meant. And I have no doubt you'll be perfect." Then her eyes widened as Violet pulled a large mahogany box from her bag. "Oooh, what's that?"

Violet slowly traced the mother-of-pearl inlay on the lid. "It's a special gift someone left for me a few months ago."

"Special gift?" Lily gave her an arch smile. "Does this mean you have an admirer?"

"Not that I know of. But it was left anonymously."

"Oh, that's even better. You can imagine the giver to be whomever or whatever you want." She held her hands out, and Violet placed the box in her grasp. "What's in it? Jewels, trinkets, perfume, a book of love poems?"

Violet laughed. "You're way off the mark. Go ahead, open it."

Lily complied, then stiffened. "A gun!"

"A very special pistol."

Lily studied it without touching it. "For a gun, it's quite pretty. That pale pink mother-of-pearl handle is nice." She glanced up. "Is it intended to be merely decorative?"

"Oh no, it works. I tried it, of course, and it shoots true." Then, as her sister recoiled, "Don't worry, it's not loaded. The bullets are safely stored in that little velvet pouch."

"What's this?" Lily lifted a small brass key that was threaded on a delicate silver chain.

"It's a key to the box." Violet shrugged. I don't keep it locked because I don't want to keep up with the key." Then she grinned, ready to share something she knew would intrigue her sister. "But the handle is only one of the things that makes the pistol special." She lowered her voice melodramatically. "It comes with a legend."

Lily's eyes lit up. "What kind of legend?"

She grinned at her sister's predictable response. "It's supposed to be a matchmaking pistol."

If anything, Lily's eyes got even wider. "Oh, this is a dilly of a gift even if it *is* a pistol. How does this matchmaking property work?"

This time Violet rolled her eyes. "Come now, you don't actually believe in this folderol, do you?"

Lily brushed aside her comment. "You didn't answer my question."

"There's a note—or series of notes, I should say—in that pocket next to the pistol. It explains everything."

Lily extracted the sheet of paper and read it out loud.

She who possesses this pistol, possesses an opportunity that must not be squandered. Cast in the tender dreams of maidens from ages past, the steel of this weapon is steadfast and true and will lead an unmarried woman to a man forged from the same virtuous elements. One need only fit her hand to the grip and open her heart to activate the promise for which this pistol was fashioned—the promise of true love. Patience and courage will illuminate her path. Hope and faith will guide her steps until her heart finds its home.

Once the promise is fulfilled, the bearer must release the pistol and pass it to another or risk losing what she has found.

Accept the gift… or not.

Believe its promise… or not.

But hoard the pistol for personal gain… and lose what you hold most dear.

Her sister lowered the note, her eyes sparkling. "But this is marvelous, a real life fairy tale."

"And just as believable," Violet said dryly.

"But all these other notes tagged onto the bottom—I mean, listen to them."

And before Violet could protest that she'd read them already, Lily enthusiastically began to read aloud once more.

Tessa James married Jackson Spivey on March 3, 1894, in Caldwell, Texas - I was aiming for his heart but accidentally winged him in the arm. Thankfully, forgiveness and love cover a multitude of mishaps.

Rena Burke wed Josh Gatlin on June 2, 1894, in Holiday, Oregon. When my trousers and target practice didn't send him running, I knew true love had hit the perfect target for me.

Kristalee Donovan wed Captain Johnny Houston on August 31, 1899, in Hugo, Indian Territory. With a little help from the pink pistol, both of us learned what love really is and will treasure that love forever. How new and bright life has suddenly become. Can there be any adventure more wonderful than this?

Goldie Colson wed Rhys Miller on August 31, 1900. I thought the pink pistol I found would save my life. It saved my heart instead. Okay, it could have saved my life too, but only because I have good aim.

Kitty Horwath married Thad Easton this 25th of December, 1910 year of our Lord. A competition in Deadwood pitted us against each other but a last-minute challenge and a test of faith won my heart (and the prize).

She dropped her hands. "Think of the history here. For the past seventeen years, this pistol has been matching couples—at least five of them. Just think, you could be number six." She breathed a happy sigh. "It's just so romantic."

Violet laughed. "Now you're just being a goof."

"Not at all. You're going to be here in town for four weeks with very little to do since your arm's in a sling. Why can't you take advantage of the legend while you're here?"

"Oh Lily, I don't know…"

"What did the note say? You fit your hand to the grip." She lifted it from its case and put action to words. "And open your heart." She held it out to Violet. "What can it hurt?"

Violet realized Lily wasn't going to let this go until she complied. So she took the pistol in hand.

"Now go ahead," Lily said. "Open your heart."

How exactly did one do that? But to appease her sister, she closed her eyes and cleared her expression. Did she want to find a steadfast and true man who would love her? Of course she did. And the note did make mention of patience and courage, hope and faith, not magic. But still, it was impossible to think the mere action of gripping the pistol would help her find her true love.

She opened her eyes to see Lily staring at her with eager anticipation. "Oh, this is going to work, I can just feel it. You must write to me as soon as you meet your true love."

"*If* I meet my true love you mean."

"You will." There was a smug certainty in Lily's voice and expression.

And for just a moment Violet allowed herself to believe.

2

As was his custom, Pastor Carson Davis rose well before sunrise and quietly dressed, then made his way to the small backyard garden where he did his morning devotions. He always felt closer to God when he was outdoors, and this morning he sorely needed the Lord's counsel. He strolled through the shadow-draped, well-manicured flower beds and fragrant crepe myrtle trees, ignoring the dew that dampened the hem of his pants. He tried to open himself up to the peace that at one time had flowed from his quiet time of morning prayer. Yet, as had been happening with increasing frequency, he found himself too distracted by other thoughts to focus.

Ever since he'd taken guardianship of Mark, he'd been praying for the wisdom and discernment to get through to the nine-year-old. And in the early weeks he'd told himself he just needed to give the boy time to mourn his mother and get accustomed to his new location and situation. But it had been almost six months now, and he hadn't made any tangible progress in building a relationship with the boy. The only thing Mark took any visible interest in were the drawings he scribbled down in his ever-present notebook. In fact, the only time he initiated any conversation was when he asked for a new notebook once the current one was filled.

Carson truly wanted to be a good father to Mark, and he was determined to make it work, to be the father figure the boy deserved and needed. He owed Mark—not to mention Mark's father—that and so much more.

It would almost be easier if Mark was a problem child—at least then he'd be able to form a plan of some sort. But Mark was polite and well-behaved, almost too much so. It seemed that his politeness was more of a wall than a bridge between them.

What did it say about his own effectiveness as a pastor if he couldn't get through to one small boy living under his roof?

Please Lord, show me the way to help this boy. I want to build a relationship with him, to have a positive impact on his life. But if that is not Your plan, if I'm not the right person to give him what he needs, show me the one who is and help me let go of my own selfish need to right a wrong so I can make that happen.

The sounds of activity in the kitchen caught his attention. Mrs. McHale, the housekeeper, was apparently at work preparing their breakfast. Looking around, he realized the sun had come up while he was focused inward.

He said one final prayer—a plea really—for wisdom and discernment in his dealings with his young charge. Then he headed back inside.

"Good morning, Mrs. McHale. Whatever you're cooking smells delicious."

"Thank you, Pastor. I plan to cook up some flapjacks with the bacon and eggs this morning. I've been thinking Mark needs a little more meat on his bones."

"That's very thoughtful of you." Not that Carson figured it

would do much good. Mark always ate what was put before him but never went back for seconds.

"It'll all work out, you'll see." The housekeeper studied him with a surprisingly knowing look. "He'll come around eventually."

She sounded a lot more sure than he felt. Then the housekeeper crossed her arms and added, "Of course, it would probably be easier on him if he had a mother in his life. And easier on you too."

Carson barely suppressed a wince. Sometimes it seemed everyone wanted to matchmake for him even though his wife had only been gone for two years. But all he said was "It's fortunate that Mark has you in his life to serve that role." Then he straightened. "I'll head on upstairs and make sure he's awake."

She turned back to the stove. "No need to rush the boy. It'll be another fifteen minutes until I have breakfast ready."

With a nod, Carson moved toward the stairs. Then he paused.

Was that his answer? Had he been pushing away the solution just because of his own unhappy experience? It wasn't as if he didn't have choices—in fact, quite the opposite. Most of the single ladies in town, as well as their matchmaking mothers, had made it obvious they would be more than happy to fill the role of pastor's wife.

Perhaps it was time he opened himself back up to the idea of marriage. But this time he'd be looking for someone to be a helpmeet in his ministry and fill the role of mother for Mark, nothing more.

"You are Lily Mayfield. You are Lily Mayfield. You *are* Lily Mayfield. You are *not* Violet Taylor."

Violet smoothed her skirt with her good hand and took a shaky breath. Even saying the litany out loud hadn't made it feel any more believable.

Would she really be able to pull this off? The plan to swap places with her twin had seemed so simple when Wyatt first concocted it. But now that he and Lily had boarded a train and left town, leaving her here with Aunt Adeline, a woman she barely knew, it no longer seemed such a good idea.

Lily had had a very genteel upbringing and worked with her great-aunt in a dress shop, working with customers and designing and creating lovely frocks. Violet had been raised on a ranch by her grandfather where she'd been surrounded by ranch hands, and nowadays she worked as a sharpshooter in a traveling show.

But she couldn't hide in Lily's bedroom all morning. Violet took a deep breath and stood. Aunt Adeline would have breakfast ready by now—she shouldn't keep her waiting.

As Violet passed the vanity that held numerous bottles filled with scents and lotions, she caught a glimpse of the solid mahogany box she'd placed front and center there last night. It looked about as out of place as a burly strongman trying to step into a graceful trapeze act.

She traced the lines of the inlay on the lid with a finger. But her thoughts were on the sheet of paper that was included with the pistol. The promise of true love—did such a thing even exist?

Violet shook off that thought and straightened. Now was not the time for such wonderings.

She quickly checked her appearance in the mirror. Since her right arm was in a sling, Aunt Adeline had helped her get dressed this morning. Her aunt had assured her this lovely green creation was one of Lily's everyday dresses, but it was fancier than anything Violet owned, including her Sunday best. She supposed working in a dress shop required one to dress fashionably. But truth to tell, with all the intricate fastenings, Violet wasn't sure she could have managed alone with two good hands. As for the deceptively easy hairstyle... She rolled her eyes. Her usual style might be plainer, but it suited her much better.

A moment later Violet slid into the dining chair across from Aunt Adeline. "Sorry if I kept you waiting."

"Nonsense. You're right on time." Aunt Adeline's soft face wore a sympathetic expression. "I know this isn't easy for you."

Violet didn't respond immediately. Instead, she studied the breakfast fare spread before her—a plate of delicate toast points, a jar of orange marmalade, two poached eggs, and juice. It was a sharp contrast to her typical breakfast of scrambled eggs, crisp bacon, sourdough biscuits, and black coffee. She reached for the glass of juice and met her aunt's gaze. "I'm worried I won't be able to pull this off."

"It's only until your arm heals—four weeks at most, you said. And I'll help you as much as I can."

She smiled at the older woman. "I appreciate that. But we both know that even though I look like Lily, I don't have her confidence, her vivaciousness. People are bound to notice."

"Perhaps. But we can blame your injury for the change in you. And besides, I think you have a spark of your own. Perhaps it's a quieter spark, but that doesn't make it any less special."

Violet fidgeted with her toast. "But I don't have Lily's ease with people. That's something you can't fake."

Aunt Adeline gave her an assessing look. "If I understand your role in that traveling circus you work at, you perform your sharpshooting act in front of throngs of people. I wouldn't think this would be very different."

"But it is. When I perform, I wear a mask so no one knows who I am—that makes it easier to be brave." She leaned forward, trying to make her aunt understand. "In my act, I'm only interacting with the target, not the people. And I know just what my role is, and I know I'm good at it."

Her companion nodded. "Well then, that's your answer. Pretend you're wearing a mask of sorts and giving a performance. Within a few days I'd be willing to wager you'll be as comfortable in this role as you are in your Masked Marvel one."

Violet thought about that as she took a bite of her poached egg. Perhaps it would help to think of this as more of a performance than the desperate move it was. She mustered up a smile. "I suppose we'll see how versatile a performer I am shortly." She dropped her gaze and fiddled with her fork. Time to change the subject. "Tell me about this pastor I'll be working with later this morning."

"Pastor Davis is a fine young man, and the congregation loves him. He's a good leader, is well spoken, compassionate, and steadfast." She tilted her head. "I take it you know Lily is smitten with him."

Violet nodded. "Do you know if those feelings are returned?" She certainly didn't want to have to try to keep up this deception in the midst of a courtship.

"Oh, I really don't think so." She pointed her fork Violet's way. "Pastor Davis is an attractive, single man with a young son. He's thirty and holds a respected position in town. Just about every eligible young lady in Larkin has her eye on him, including your sister."

He was attractive, was he? "With all those qualifications, it's surprising he hasn't married already."

Her aunt sobered. "He was once. I hear his wife died about two years ago from a fever."

"Oh, that's awful." Was he still nursing a broken heart?

Her aunt's expression took on a slightly cynical twist. "That tragic history also serves to make him more attractive to soft-hearted, romantic-minded young ladies." Then she smiled. "Not that he appears to have let it go to his head. He's always the perfect gentleman and never seems to show a preference for one lady over another. Including Lily, I'm afraid."

Rather than respond to that, Violet shifted the focus. "So he's had to raise his son without a wife."

"Oh no, Mark's not actually his son. In fact, Mark has only been living with him for about six months, which was when his mother died. I believe the pastor was a friend of the boy's father."

They must have been good friends indeed for him, a single man, to take guardianship of his child. And this was the man she was going to try to convince that she was Lily.

After breakfast, they headed downstairs where Aunt Adeline immediately went to the shop windows and raised the shades. The sun beamed through the windows, highlighting the colorful frocks and fabrics like jewels in a treasure chest.

Then her aunt went to the shop door and, with her hand on the lock, turned to Violet. "Ready?"

Violet's stomach fluttered in protest, but she nodded.

"Good girl." And with an approving smile, Aunt Adeline unlocked the door and turned the CLOSED sign in the window to OPEN.

The seasoned dressmaker had barely taken three steps back toward the counter when the shop bell chimed as the door opened. Her aunt immediately turned and stepped up to greet the two customers who'd entered. "Mavis, Susan, how are you ladies this morning?"

The older woman, possibly the mother of the other, much younger lady, answered first. "We're quite well. But Susan needs a new Sunday dress."

"Of course." She led the ladies to the far wall where bolts of fabric were shelved.

Susan, who lagged behind, turned to greet Violet, then

stopped as her eyes widened in concern. "Lily! What happened to your arm?"

Violet gave what she hoped was a believable grimace. "Nothing exciting, I'm afraid. Just me being clumsy. I fell and managed to sprain my wrist." Which was entirely true.

That didn't seem to relieve Susan's concern. "Oh my goodness. I hope it isn't painful."

"Right now it's more an annoyance than pain. I'm afraid I'm not going to be of much help to Aunt Adeline for a few weeks."

"Nonsense, my dear." Aunt Adeline had decided to join the conversation. "I told you we'd manage just fine." She turned to Mavis. "In fact, I wanted her to stay upstairs and take it easy today, but she insisted on coming down to help out."

"Commendable." Then Mavis turned back to Aunt Adeline without giving Violet another glance. "Now about that fabric you wanted to show me?"

Violet's aunt was all business once more as she nodded and led the women across the room.

Too full of nervous energy to stand still, Violet decided it would be a good idea to at least pretend to be busy. So she retrieved a feather duster she'd spotted behind the counter and began fussily dusting display tables and notion racks. She'd taken the time after the Emporium closed the prior evening to familiarize herself with the layout of the shop and the items offered. But it wouldn't hurt to go over it again.

On one of the shelves she spotted some lovely pink mother-of-pearl buttons. She picked one up between two fingers, studying how pretty it looked in the sunlight streaming in through the window. It brought her thoughts back around to the contents of the box on the vanity table upstairs. It was such a strange keepsake, if that's what one could call it. The idea of a pistol having some sort of mystical matchmaking properties was ridiculous. Still, there was some small part of her that wanted to believe...

Which only served to prove how foolish she was. She firmly set the button down and moved on to the next bin.

A quick glance at the clock was enough to agitate the butterflies in her stomach again. In just a little over an hour, she'd have her first real test of her ability to pull off posing as Lily. She'd be facing a room full of the children Lily had been working with for weeks, as well as the pastor who'd known Lily for over a year. And she wouldn't have Aunt Adeline to come to her rescue if she ran into trouble. At least she wouldn't need to worry about having to face the parents as well. When Lily told her what to expect from the children, she'd mentioned that no one, not even the moms and dads, were allowed to watch the practice sessions. The official reason was so the parents could be surprised with everyone else the day of the performance. But it was also so the adults wouldn't make the children nervous or try to "help" with the direction.

To be honest, she'd much rather face a crowd filled with hecklers as the Masked Marvel than try to make her vivacious sister's friends believe she was Lily.

And the thought of messing up Lily's chances of gaining the pastor's favor was downright gut-clenching. Her best course of action would be to focus on the practice itself, to interact with the pastor as little as possible and leave as quickly as possible.

And reading between the lines from Lily's letters and her aunt's comments, that shouldn't be very much of a problem. The pastor seemed to be all business with little interest in responding to any advances made to engage his affections.

She'd be okay as long as she used her arm as an excuse not to be very sociable.

Wouldn't she?

3

"Have you reconsidered your decision not to be part of the church program?"

Carson and Mark strolled down the sidewalk, heading for the church. There was a practice session scheduled for the children's program later this morning, and he'd asked the boy to accompany him. As usual, Mark had nodded politely, closed his notebook, and stood.

"No, sir."

Always the shortest, unemotional answer.

"Do you mind if I ask why?" If there was some way to get Mark interested in interacting with the other children rather than just sketching all the time, it might help the boy to build relationships with his peers.

Mark shrugged. "I don't think I'd like it."

Carson tried to tamp down his frustration and maintain an even, pleasant tone. "If you're afraid you won't be good at it, I'm sure all you'd need is a bit of practice to fit in with the others. And I know they would all be willing to help you."

Again the boy shrugged, but this time he didn't say anything.

Carson smothered a sigh and faced forward. Time to mentally prepare for the upcoming practice. The church's twenty-fifth-anniversary celebration was just three weeks away, and they still had a lot of work to do to get ready.

He expected Lily Mayfield to be there when he arrived. He worked with the children who were participating in the short play from nine thirty to ten thirty, and Lily had the children's choir from ten thirty until eleven thirty. But they always sat in on each other's sessions to assist and provide suggestions and advice. And she usually showed up ten or fifteen minutes early, finding reasons to speak to him before the children arrived.

His thoughts went back to his new perspective on marriage. One of the primary attributes he'd be looking for was a strong, loving, motherly instinct. That really wasn't the first thing that came to mind when he thought of the young seamstress.

Not that there was anything in Miss Mayfield that he found particularly objectionable, quite the opposite actually. There was much to admire about her—she was exuberant, generous, lighthearted. She made folks feel good just to be around her.

Since he wasn't necessarily looking for a love match, perhaps he needed to look at her with fresh eyes.

Her, along with several other young ladies in the community.

"LET'S TAKE A SHORT BREAK, and then we'll go over the closing scene one more time."

Carson made a few notes on his copy of the script. Henry must have been practicing at home because he definitely showed some improvement. But Joey was still having problems with his lines. Carson really didn't want to replace the boy, but he might need to have him swap roles with someone who had much fewer lines. He'd need to make that decision quickly though.

Carson looked at his pocket watch and was surprised to see it was ten fifteen. Where was Miss Mayfield? Much as he mentally rolled his eyes over her little flirtations, it seemed her presence had become something he almost unconsciously relied on, the way one relied on the chimes of a grandfather clock to mark the hour. And he would actually like to get her perspective on the situation with Joey.

Of all days for her to be late. Perhaps she'd just gotten busy at the dress shop.

He cast a quick glance Mark's way. The boy had his head down and was studiously sketching. How could he possibly have so many different things to draw?

Clapping his hands, he called the children back together. They'd just gotten started when he heard a soft cough from somewhere at the back of the church. He glanced around and was surprised to see Miss Mayfield seated in a far corner almost lost in shadow. How long had she been there? And why hadn't she come right up front as she normally did?

Not wanting to interrupt their practice time, Carson decided those questions could wait. He turned back to the group. "All right. Lizzie and Henry, let's pick things up from the part where the two of you place the books on the shelves."

For some reason, having Lily Mayfield watch from the back of the church made him self-conscious where having her up front never had. Or perhaps it was this whole finding-a-wife thing.

He was distracted to the point that he finally ended practice five minutes early. "I think we'll stop here. You all did well, but be sure you practice your lines whenever you can. And I'll see you back here on Thursday."

As the young cast gathered up their things and headed for

the exit, Carson turned to where he'd spotted Miss Mayfield earlier. She was now surrounded by the half dozen or so children who had already arrived for choir practice.

It was only when she stood that he spotted the sling. No wonder she was off her usual routine this morning.

He crossed the distance between them quickly. "Miss Mayfield, you're injured. What happened?"

She waved her good hand dismissively. "No need to worry, Pastor Davis. It was just a silly trip and fall, nothing serious. Doc said I should be as good as new in a few weeks."

Pastor Davis? She usually used the more familiar Pastor Carson. And most people here used Dr. Martin's full title. "Are you certain you're all right? Shouldn't you be at home resting?"

She tucked a stray tendril behind her ear and bit her lip, her glance shying away from his.

Was she embarrassed by her accident?

"You're kind to be so concerned," she continued, "but I'm fine. I didn't intend to interrupt your practice session."

He waved aside her concern. "We were nearly finished anyway." The door opened again as several of the children made their exits and others arrived.

She picked up her tote bag and slipped out of the pew. "I suppose I should get things set up for choir practice."

"Allow me," he said as he took the tote from her. "And I'll certainly add a request for healing grace for you in my prayers."

"Thank you." And with a quick smile, she continued down the aisle without waiting for him to accompany her.

He rubbed his jaw as he followed more slowly. There was something different about her this morning. Her conversation had lacked its usual coquettish warmth. In fact, she'd almost seemed eager to distance herself. It could be because of her injury he supposed. Still, he sensed there was something more.

After setting her tote where she could get to it easily, he slid into the second pew and watched her greet the children as they arrived. There was still that air of tentativeness about her. Had the accident sobered her, made her feel more unsure of herself?

Then to his surprise, a few minutes before it was time to start, Miss Mayfield moved over to Mark, who sat at the other end of his pew. Surprising because while she'd always made a point to greet Mark, she'd otherwise left him alone ever since he'd said he wasn't interested in singing with the children's choir. He couldn't keep himself from eavesdropping on their conversation.

Her opening wasn't very auspicious. "Do you mind if I have a look at your drawings?"

Predictably Mark stiffened and gave her a suspicious look. For a long moment he didn't respond to her request.

Carson tensed. Surely he wouldn't outright refuse.

But then Miss Mayfield gave the boy a sympathetic smile. "It's okay if you'd rather not. I know there are some things you want to hold on to just for yourself. I have some things like that myself."

Her words were soft, barely carrying to Carson, and he suddenly wanted to know what she was referring to.

Mark relaxed and nodded. He dropped his gaze and twisted his pencil between his fingers.

She tapped her chin with an index finger, studying him. "I know you don't want to participate in the program, but I wonder if you wouldn't mind helping me out today." She raised the elbow of her injured limb. "With my arm in this sling, I won't be able to both direct and hold the music."

The boy hesitated for just a second, then nodded. He carefully set his closed notebook and pencil down and stood.

Miss Mayfield gave him a bright smile, then led the way back to the front. "All right, children, I think we're all here now. Let's start with 'What a Friend We Have in Jesus' today. Everyone, take your places."

Concerned that she wasn't quite herself and might need more of a helping hand than Mark could provide, Carson cleared his throat. "If you think you'll need some additional help, I'd be glad to offer my services."

She gave him a polite smile. "That's not necessary. I'm sure Mark and the other children will provide any assistance I need."

Not the reaction he'd expected. He pulled out the small notebook and pencil that he always kept in his jacket pocket. "Very well. I can work on Sunday's sermon. But I'll be here if you need me." He turned to his notebook. But not before he noticed the uncertain expression on her face. It was almost as if she'd rather he not be there.

But he put those thoughts aside as he watched the easy way she was able to draw Mark out. She smiled and spoke with the boy but didn't make a big show of it. He couldn't make out what she said to him, but her gentle tone and expressions of approval seemed to coax Mark into offering his opinion—something he himself had never been able to do.

Lily had always had a talent for making people feel comfortable, but this was different. This wasn't the effervescent, confident, take-charge woman who'd been working with these children for the past three weeks. Instead, Miss Mayfield seemed more observant, more attuned to the individual children in the group. She was trying a different, softer approach this morning, and the children seemed to relax, drawn in by her gentle leadership and attentive responses. Even when things didn't go as planned—which happened often enough this morning with her decreased mobility—she kept everyone encouraged with smiles and a self-deprecating attitude of understanding.

He made a few notes on next Sunday's sermon, but his eyes were constantly drawn back to her.

When practice was over, he made his way to the front, adding his congratulations to the children for how well they'd done and wishing them good day.

When everyone but Mark and Miss Mayfield had gone, he turned to the boy. "Mark, you did a good job helping Miss Mayfield today. I'm proud of you."

If he'd expected Mark's attitude toward him to have warmed, he was disappointed. The boy's only response was a nod, and his demeanor was as polite and withdrawn as ever. He turned and walked away to retrieve his notebook and pencil.

Carson held on to his smile. "If you don't mind waiting for me in the office, I'd like to have a word with Miss Mayfield."

"Yes, sir." And without another word or change of expression, Mark turned and headed toward the side door.

VIOLET WATCHED the exchange between the two with sympathy. There seemed to be a bit of stiffness between the pastor and his charge. She wished she could do something to help them. She had some experience with how it felt to lose your parents and then be sent to live with people she barely knew in a place far from where she'd been raised. Mark was no doubt hurting no matter how placid his outward appearance.

Then she realized the pastor had turned back to her. What did he want to speak to her about? Her stomach clenched, and her palms suddenly felt moist. Had he already seen through her deception? She should have known she couldn't fool anyone into believing she was Lily without Aunt Adeline there to help cover for her.

"I know you said you weren't feeling any ill effects from your accident, but are you sure it's not too soon for you to be taxing yourself this way?" His expression had a serious, concerned look to it.

Uh-oh, he'd no doubt noticed how she'd forgotten or mixed up a child's name a time or two. And Lily had forgotten to tell her about a slight change she'd made to one of the songs. She'd hoped she'd managed to laugh those off convincingly but apparently not. Her only choice was to use the blame-it-on-the-injury excuse. "I know I seemed more distracted than usual today, but I assure you I'm fine. And by Thursday's session I should be more clearheaded."

"I'm glad to hear it." His tone didn't sound entirely convinced. But after another probing look, he changed the subject. "I also wanted to thank you for what you did today with Mark."

Her tension eased somewhat as sympathy took its place.

"I've been trying to get him to open up and really talk to me for months now, and I haven't had much luck. But today…" He tugged on his cuff. "You were able to get him to actually engage with you in a way that I haven't seen him do since he moved in with me."

Violet felt a warmth spread through her chest at his words, but she tried to brush off his thanks. "I didn't really do anything much. I just talked to him like I would any of the children."

"Well, whatever you did, it apparently did the trick." The pastor looked back in the direction Mark had exited, and the pensive expression that crossed his face made her want to offer a sympathetic touch.

Instead, she settled for words. "I'm sure he'll open up to you in time."

The pastor seemed to pull himself back together. "Yes, of course. So let's talk about today's performances. I'm not sure when you arrived—did you see how much Joey is still struggling?"

She assumed Joey was the boy who had the role of mayor. "Yes, and I have an idea. As I was reading through the script, I realized that some of Joey's lines aren't necessary or can be shortened to get the same point across." She was attempting to pull a folder from her tote as she spoke.

"Here, let me." He retrieved the folder she'd been struggling with.

She gave him a smile of thanks and then sat on the pew and opened the folder in her lap. "I made some notes on the script to give you an idea of what I was thinking." She handed it back to him with an apologetic grimace. "You may not be able to read it. I had to do it with my left hand."

He took a look at her notes. As she'd warned, it was difficult to read, but he was able to make out enough of it to see what she meant. "You're right. This will be much easier for Joey to work with and nothing of import is lost. I'm not sure why I didn't see this sooner."

She made a dismissive gesture. "It's always easier to see these sorts of things when you're looking at it with fresh eyes."

"Fresh eyes?"

She mentally kicked herself. Why couldn't she think before she spoke? "I mean looking at it specifically to find ways to make it easier to help Joey."

He nodded, but she still saw a question in his gaze.

She put on her most innocent expression. "I don't think it will shorten the length of the play as a whole, do you?"

"A few minutes here or there won't be a problem. Especially since there may be a few unexpected pauses along the way." He closed the folder. "If you'll allow me to take this with me, I'll make the changes and deliver the new lines to Joey this afternoon."

Happy he didn't seem ready to press her on her missteps, Violet gave him a broad smile. "Of course. I'm hopeful this will make it an easier target for him to hit now."

He raised a brow but nodded. "Tell me, how do you think the children are doing overall—both your group and mine? Do you think they'll be ready for the performance in three weeks' time?"

That was a question she didn't have to give a lot of thought to. "I do. They may not be perfect, but from what I've seen, they'll definitely be giving the audience their best effort." Then she lifted her chin. "And I find that it's often the little mistakes that turn out to be what makes a performance memorable."

His lips twitched. "That's a rather unique way of looking at it."

"Perhaps, but true nonetheless."

"I agree."

For some reason his answer and his approving smile lightened her mood.

But best not to press her luck—no need to give him more reasons to wonder about the change in her. "If there's nothing else, I need to get back to the Emporium. I should be there to help Aunt Adeline." Then she smiled and raised her injured arm slightly. "As much as I can at any rate."

"Of course." The pastor reached for her tote bag. "Here let me help you with that."

She held out her good hand to take it from him.

But rather than handing it to her, he met her gaze. "Would you like me to carry this for you?"

She kept her hand outstretched. "That's not necessary. I carried it here, I can carry it back."

Something flickered in his gaze—was it surprise? But he merely nodded. "Very well. I'll see you Thursday. I hope your arm is much improved by then."

"Thank you." And with a quick nod she hurried down the aisle and out of the building.

Violet took a deep breath as she closed the church door behind her. Had she done enough to ease Pastor Davis's suspicions? It had been her first real test, and she'd been so nervous. Which had no doubt played into her performance. She had the feeling he had noted something wrong, but hopefully he put it down to her injury. She'd have to be more careful next time.

Then she grimaced. She hated all this pretense—she might as well have lied outright.

It made it even worse that she was trying to deceive a man of God. Why oh why had she let Wyatt talk her into this?

As she moved down the sidewalk, she felt some of her tension ease. Being outdoors always gave her a sense of freedom and possibilities, especially when she was on her own without the weight of someone else's judgment or expectations weighing her down.

Surely the worst was behind her. Thank goodness Lily had done such a good job describing each of the children and their roles in the performance. There'd only been once when she'd messed up—a few more if you counted the times she'd had to correct herself—but hopefully none of the children had noticed, except perhaps Mark. She could tell there was keen intelligence behind his unconcerned air, and she got the sense he didn't miss much. Having him help her out had been an impulsive gesture, one brought on by the fact that she could sense a kindred soul in him. He had that closed-off air that reminded her of herself during those early days after her parents died. Did the pastor understand what the boy was going through? Would he welcome her thoughts on the matter, or would he see it as unwanted meddling in a private matter?

Whatever the case, she'd do what she could to help Mark in the short time she would be here.

Which led her thoughts to Pastor Davis himself. She could see why Lily was drawn to the man. He had a presence about him, an air of authority mixed with service to others that was very attractive. But there was more than that. On a personal level he seemed kind and genuinely concerned about her injury. She'd done her absolute best not to lie to him outright, but she was miserably aware that a lie of omission was still a lie.

"Lily."

It took Violet a moment to realize she was being hailed. She turned to see a plump woman with mud-brown hair done up in tortuous curls and a determined expression lurking behind her too-bright smile. Oh dear, who was this woman and what did she want with Lily?

Not sure if this was friend or foe, Violet gave her a tentative smile. "Yes?"

The woman's gaze latched onto the sling cradling Violet's right arm. "Whatever did you do to yourself?"

"I sprained my wrist. It's nothing serious."

"Oh well, that's a relief." The woman seemed to completely erase the injury from her consciousness. "I wanted to check in and see how the program is coming along. My Dorey has been practicing nonstop so that she can do her best when it comes time for the show, and I'm sure you'll agree she will be a shining star among them all!"

Her mind scrambled to dredge up an image of Dorey. Then she remembered—a sweet little seven-year-old with a lovely voice. "Dorey is indeed quite talented."

The woman nodded, her expression smug. "It would be even more special if she could do a solo, don't you think?"

Violet was taken aback for a moment. This woman obviously knew Lily at least well enough to approach her with such a bold request, but how would her sister respond? Regardless, Violet couldn't in good conscience agree to such a thing.

Time to be diplomatic. "Dorey will have an important role to play, as will each of the children," Violet said carefully. "We're doing our best to give everyone a chance to shine in their own way."

Mrs. Lundell gave her a probing look. Then she nodded,

although something in her expression told Violet she wasn't entirely convinced. "Of course," she said with a forced smile before turning to go. "You are in charge after all."

With a nod, Violet once again headed toward the Emporium. She would have to ask Aunt Adeline about the woman.

As she continued on her way, she thought about the children she'd just spent an hour with. The things Lily had told her about them had helped her work with them today. It was obvious they were excited about the program, and while some were more talented than others, she was determined to make sure they all felt comfortable and prepared.

As for Mark, she had the glimmer of an idea about how she could draw him into the group a little better. She'd have to give it some more thought but would hopefully be able to speak to the pastor about it Thursday.

She had a few more encounters before she reached the Emporium, mostly people inquiring about her injury, but to her relief, she was able to navigate through them without any missteps.

4

A fter watching Miss Mayfield make her exit, Carson
headed for the church office.

Mark was there, not surprisingly with his head
bent over his notebook. But for some reason Carson had the
feeling that he'd just turned from staring out the window.
Glancing that way himself, Carson spotted two boys about
Mark's age taking advantage of the glorious weather, playing
tag while a floppy-eared dog ran from one to the other.

Did Mark wish he was out there playing with them? "I see
Ralph and Danny outside," he said casually. "If you'd like to
join them, you're welcome to."

Mark barely looked up. "No, thank you."

Carson dropped into his chair. "I have a few things to take
care of here. You can wait with me or head home. Mrs.
McHale should have lunch ready shortly."

"Is it all right if I take the long way?"

Carson knew Mark liked to take walks to find subjects for
his drawings. "Yes, but don't stray too far and make sure
you're home in time for lunch."

With a nod the boy closed his notebook and left the room.

Carson hadn't missed the involuntary wince that crossed Mark's face at the word *home.*

Lord, please give me patience to wait on Your timing and the faith to believe You are at work here. And show me the way to help Mark find joy in living again.

Then he leaned back in his chair and thought about all that had occurred this morning. Miss Mayfield had obviously made a connection of sorts with Mark today. He'd actually seen the boy smile at one of her self-deprecating comments earlier. He wasn't sure why that had happened today when the two had never shown any sort of connection before. Perhaps it was nothing more than the dressmaker's sling, which gave her an air of vulnerability. Or maybe it was because he had determined to make himself open to the idea of finding a wife.

Would he also find himself seeing other candidates in a better light?

That question was put to the test twenty minutes later as he and Mark headed home to eat lunch.

They had crossed half the distance when he saw Jenny Filmore approaching from the opposite direction, a shopping bag on her arm. Miss Filmore was one of several young ladies who had made their interest in him clear over the past year.

As he had with Miss Mayfield this morning, Carson forced himself not to immediately put his guard up but to allow himself to see whatever good qualities she might have as a mother for Mark.

As soon as she neared, Miss Filmore stopped and greeted him with a flashy, flirtatious smile. "Good afternoon, Pastor. Isn't it a beautiful day?"

Carson nodded in acknowledgment. "It certainly is that. I hope your parents are well."

She preened slightly. "They are, thank you." Then she turned to Mark. "Hello, young man. You certainly are looking handsome today."

Mark looked uncomfortable as he murmured a hello in response. Had he also heard the effusive condescension in her tone?

Miss Filmore, however, seemed oblivious to Mark's reaction. "Always so shy," she continued brightly. "But I'm sure you'll get over that someday." Then she cast a coquettish look his way. "You certainly have a good example to learn from in the pastor."

Carson saw Mark pull further back into himself as she spoke. It was time to put an end to the boy's discomfort. "You'll have to excuse us." He maintained a polite smile but kept his tone firm. "Mark and I are on our way home to have lunch. Please give your parents my regards."

"Of course. And I look forward to your sermon on Sunday."

As they moved away from Miss Filmore, he sensed an easing of Mark's tension. That touched something protective and almost paternal inside Carson.

The difference in the way Miss Filmore had interacted with Mark just now and the way Lily Mayfield had earlier today was like night and day.

Yesterday she'd been just another member of his congregation, admittedly engaging and pleasing to be around but not anyone who tempted him to give up his bachelor status.

Today, with his new willingness to seek out a mother for Mark, she had become the standard he gauged the candidates for wife by.

What a difference a day made.

AUNT ADELINE FLIPPED the sign in the window to CLOSED and locked the door. Then she turned to Violet with a smile. "We haven't had such a busy afternoon at the Emporium since the

Morgans decided to hold a formal Christmas party. But I do believe at least half our customers came by to see your arm in that sling rather than to place an order."

"Glad I could provide your neighbors with some entertainment," Violet said dryly as she pulled down one of the shades.

"You handled yourself well. I don't think anyone suspects." She smiled innocently. "And I may have planted a few seeds that you've been distracted and not quite yourself since your accident."

Violet rolled her eyes as she closed the second shade.

"I need to make some alterations to Molly Saunders's dress." Aunt Adeline moved toward the workroom. "Do you mind helping me?"

"I'll be glad to." Violet lifted the elbow of her injured arm. "As much as I'm able anyway."

Her aunt grinned. "Other than some occasional fetching or handing me things, I'm actually more interested in having your company than your assistance."

"That I can do." Violet followed the dressmaker into the workroom.

Once her aunt had settled herself in front of the dress form holding the tailored powder-blue-and-ivory dress, she opened the conversation. "So tell me how it went at the church this morning."

Violet handed her some pins. "The children were great to work with. And I don't think they noticed anything different about me personally." She grinned. "They were too interested in my sling to really notice anything else."

"And how did it go with Pastor Davis?" Her aunt's tone was just a little too casual.

Violet brushed at her skirt to give herself time to form an answer. "He showed concern when he saw my injury."

Her aunt actually rolled her eyes. "Of course he did. He's a compassionate man. What I meant was, did he show any indication he suspected you weren't Lily?"

"I'm pretty sure he realized something wasn't quite right." She remembered that puzzled look on his face when she'd first addressed him. It was only later she remembered Lily referred to him as Pastor Carson rather than Pastor Davis. She changed the subject. "Has Mark always been so distant?"

The older woman nodded sadly. "I'm afraid the boy hasn't adjusted to life here very well. The poor thing is probably still mourning the loss of his mother."

"What about his father?"

"I heard he'd passed away several years ago while Mark was still quite young." Then she met Violet's gaze. "Is there a reason for this interest in Mark? He's not in the choir is he?"

"No. But he just looked so lost, like he needed a friend."

Her aunt's expression softened. "You're a good person."

She didn't feel like a good person. But she brushed that aside.

There was a pause in the conversation as the dressmaker placed some pins in the garment. When she spoke up again, she changed the subject. "Tell me something about how you grew up and how you ended up in a traveling show as a sharpshooter."

So for the next thirty minutes, Violet told her aunt about her life on her grandfather's ranch. How her grandfather had bitterly blamed her father for taking his daughter so far from him and ultimately for her mother's death. It was why he'd changed her surname to match his.

Other than school and church, she didn't get to town much growing up. Her only real companion had been Wyatt, the son of her grandfather's housekeeper.

She also told how her grandfather had taught her to hunt and shoot, and it turned out she had a real knack for it.

Violet paused and realized she'd been rambling and had said a lot more than she intended to. What must her aunt think?

"That's an interesting way to grow up. Like Mark, it must have taken you time to adapt."

Interesting? She supposed it could be looked at that way. "Yes, but eventually I did." She fiddled with her collar, not quite meeting her aunt's gaze. "I imagine it was very different from the way Lily grew up. But I learned to love my grandfather, and I had so much freedom to explore and do things I'd never have had the opportunity to do in what you might call a normal setting."

"Well, there you have it." Her aunt sat back and studied her work critically, then gave Violet a sunny smile. "Your upbringing turned you into the unique, sweet person you are today, so no matter how different it was, one can't find fault with it."

Feeling better but not sure how to respond to that, Violet held her peace.

"This talent you have with a gun," her aunt said after a moment, "is that how you got involved with the circus?"

"Sort of. When my granddad passed away, I couldn't hold on to the ranch. There was a traveling show passing through town at the time, and Wyatt came up with the idea of the two of us joining."

"How old were you at the time?"

"Sixteen."

Her aunt paused in her work and captured Violet's gaze with a very direct look. "Tell me, what is it you want for your life?"

Violet was taken aback at the abrupt change of subject. "What do you mean?"

"It sounds to me as if up to this point you've had other people directing the course of your life. Your grandfather whisked you away when your parents died and did his best to erase all evidence of your father's life from your own, including your sister. You just said it was Wyatt's idea for you two to join the traveling show in the first place. And when you arrived here, you mentioned Wyatt came up with the plan for this swap of identities." She held up a hand. "I know not all of those decisions were bad. With the exception of some of the things your grandfather decided for you, those were likely necessary solutions to your needs at the time. But I am saying things are different now. For one thing, you have me and Lily to fall back on if you need time to think things through. We may all be women, but we're strong women and we pull together for each other. We're family."

"I consider Wyatt family. He's always done what he thinks is best for me. And remember, he's the one who found you and Lily so that we could be reunited."

"Of course, dear. I didn't mean to imply he wasn't. And I will be forever grateful that he did find and contact us. But you're at a crossroads of sorts now. Which means you have options you didn't have before. So, I guess my question is, do you enjoy performing in the traveling show? Is that something you want to continue for years to come? If so, that's perfectly all right as long as you keep in touch. But if there's something else you'd like to do with your life, then that's all right too. Whatever you decide, Lily and I will be here to provide as much or as little help as you need."

Violet wasn't sure what to say. Sure, she'd always wondered what it would be like to be what her grandfather called a townie. Twice before in her life she'd left everything familiar behind to start over in what was essentially a new world. It hadn't been easy either time.

Did she really want to do that again?

Aunt Adeline interrupted her thoughts. "I don't expect you to answer me, dear, especially right now. I just wanted to make sure you thought about it while you're here."

To her relief, her aunt stood and began putting away her pins and scissors. "But enough of this. I'll save the rest of my questions for another time." She headed for the workroom door. "Let's go upstairs. And while I prepare supper, I'll tell you some stories about Lily's childhood."

5

Later that evening when she'd retired to her room, Violet threw her window open as far as she could and leaned out, inhaling the fresh night air and staring up at the almost-full moon. She'd made it through her first day with only a few missteps. How was Lily doing? Was she finding it difficult to navigate life in a traveling show, or was she breezing through it as she seemed to do with other aspects of her life?

Violet rested her head against the window frame and thought about her aunt's words again.

What *did* she want for her life?

Life with the traveling show had been good to her. It had given her a home, a place to belong, and a way to earn a living when she'd had nowhere else to go. She'd had an opportunity to see parts of the country she likely wouldn't have otherwise. And it had also given her a sense of pride for a skill most folks might have looked down on in a woman.

But was it really how she wanted to spend the rest of her life? And if she left the show, what would that mean for Wyatt? He'd given up so much to make sure she was safe and secure. If she left, would he come with her? Or did he actually like performing in the show? Strange that she didn't know the answer to that last question.

Then there was the question of where she would go and what she would do. She certainly wouldn't want to live off her aunt's charity, but was she qualified to do anything besides fire a gun with pinpoint accuracy? And that wasn't a skill that was in high demand, especially for a young lady.

As Aunt Adeline said, she didn't have to decide today. But she owed it to herself to take advantage of these next four weeks to figure it out.

She went to the vanity and lifted the mahogany box and set it on the bed beside her.

When she'd first found it in the small closet-of-a-room she used for changing, she thought it was a mistake. But the package was addressed to the Masked Marvel. So she'd opened it and been entranced by the beauty and craftsmanship that had gone into the creation of the solid but somehow feminine weapon. When she'd picked it up, it fit her hand perfectly and her mind had gone immediately to how she could showcase it in her act.

Then she'd found the note tucked inside and her view of the gift had shifted. Was she actually supposed to believe the pistol had some kind of matchmaking properties?

Still, it had found its way into the hands of at least five women who had believed exactly that if the additional lines penned beneath the legend were any indication. Apparently the last person on that list thought she was in need of some matchmaking help since they'd passed it on to her. Which might be true but it still didn't sit well with her that she was perceived that way.

Of course she didn't believe in such mystic nonsense. That's why she'd returned the pistol and note to their box and stuffed it down in the trunk that held most of her earthly possessions. She hadn't told anyone, not even Wyatt. Until Lily had asked about it. Funny how Lily's bubbly enthusiasm for the legend and willingness to believe had been almost contagious.

Because she might not believe in the pistol's matchmaking properties, but the promise the note held was alluring nonetheless. Growing up she hadn't had much chance to court or be courted. Living on her grandfather's ranch she'd been rather isolated. And after she and Wyatt had joined the travelling show, Wyatt had made it clear she was under his protection.

Besides all that, she led too unorthodox a life for any respectable man to want to court her.

Then again, no one here knew any of that history...

VIOLET SPENT most of the next morning behind the counter in the dress shop. Business was slow today, and Aunt Adeline was able to handle most of the customers that did show up. Violet was only called on to assist once, and that was to help a young lady choose some lace for a dress she was making herself.

She had spent a lot of time after she'd turned in last night thinking about the question her aunt had posed and about the promise of the pink pistol. Her grandfather had had very little use for townies and the kind of life they lived. And later her circus friends had had similar attitudes. She'd never really questioned it. But last night she'd searched her memories of those early days when her family had still been intact. There weren't many specifics—playing with Lily, being rocked to sleep by her mother, hugged by her father after a fall. But the overall feelings they gave her were of happiness and security. Before she'd drifted off to sleep, she'd finally decided that she owed it to herself to give this townie life a genuine chance.

This morning though, her thoughts had turned to the pastor and his young ward. Mark needed some help to find his place in his new world. He seemed even more withdrawn than she herself had been in her early days at the ranch. But she'd had Wyatt to help her.

She sensed Pastor Davis—no, Pastor Carson—understood Mark was hurting and sincerely wanted to help the boy but he just hadn't had any success yet. She hoped that meant he would be receptive to her idea.

The shop bell rang, and Violet pasted on her "Welcome, customer" smile as she turned to see who had entered. To her surprise, it was Pastor Carson. What in creation was he doing in a dress shop?

Aunt Adeline was working with another customer, so Violet stepped around the counter to greet him. "Pastor Carson, is there something I can help you with?"

He didn't seem to feel at all out of place. "I hope so. I was wondering if your aunt could spare you for a short while. There's a matter about the children I'd like to discuss with you."

After the way she'd messed things up yesterday, Violet wasn't sure she was ready to be alone with him right now. Deciding to give the townie life a fighting chance didn't mean she should risk messing things up for Lily.

But apparently Aunt Adeline had been listening because she replied before Violet could. "Of course, Pastor. Go on along, Lily."

He smiled at the older woman. "Thank you, Mrs. Clemmons. I promise I won't keep her long."

Aunt Adeline waved a hand. "No need to rush. Take whatever time you need."

Violet tried to find a middle ground. "We could talk here. That way I could help Aunt Adeline if she needs me."

Aunt Adeline spoke up again. "Nonsense. I'll be fine." Her gaze met Violet's with a very strong *go* message.

Violet knew when she was defeated. "If you're sure." She turned back to the pastor. "It seems I'm at your service."

With a nod he gestured toward the door. "Shall we go for a walk?"

Violet brushed at her skirt and allowed him to lead her from the shop.

CARSON HAD the distinct impression she hadn't wanted to leave the shop. Why? Was it because she didn't want to leave her aunt as she'd stated? Or did it have something to do with him?

Apparently he'd spent too much time mulling that over because she finally spoke up, prompting him to get down to business.

"Where's Mark this morning?"

"He's at home with Mrs. McHale." Drawing in his notebook no doubt. "In fact, he's actually who I want to discuss with you."

"So it's not about the church program."

"Not exactly."

"Well, I'm happy to help however I can."

"I assume you've noticed that Mark keeps to himself quite a bit?"

Her smile turned sympathetic as she nodded. "Yes, I imagine he's still in mourning."

"But yesterday you managed to draw him out in a way I haven't been able to do since he moved in with me. I guess I'd like to know if you can explain to me how you did it so I can try to replicate it."

She hesitated a moment, then gave a self-deprecating smile. "I saw myself in him."

He felt his brow furrow. "I'm not sure I understand."

"I reckon you wouldn't have reason to know this, but I was also orphaned as a child." She waved her free hand. "I just realized I ought to draw on my own experience to understand what he's going through, what he might need."

He knew Lily's parents were no longer around, but he'd never heard the details. But while he was trying to decide if he should ask, she continued.

"In my case I was five. And I was put in the care of grandparents I barely knew. I was moved from my home and all the people and places I knew, even my own sister."

"You have a sister?" That surprised him more than the other details.

Some strong emotion crossed her expression at that, and she looked away as she nodded. What was the story there?

But rather than expanding on that point, she continued her explanation. "I know now that everyone just did what they thought best for me, but back then—when my grief and fear were so new and almost a physical pain—it felt like an additional punishment."

He tried to absorb everything she'd just said. "I'm sorry. That must have been a terrible time for you." Lily had never seemed so vulnerable before. And all the more so because he didn't hear any self-pity in her tone.

Her smile did nothing to hide the incredible sadness reflected in her eyes. "I survived. But I had a friend, a boy a few years older than me, who was relentless about trying to draw me out."

He was glad to hear she'd had that at least. "Unfortunately, Mark doesn't seem interested in making friends here, not even when school was in session." Her perspective had been very helpful though.

They were nearing Mickelson's Bakery and the door opened, allowing a young lady to step out. He had to swallow a groan when he realized it was Jenny Filmore.

Upon spotting them, she gave him a broad smile. "Pastor Carson, how are you?" The smile she gave his companion was not quite so bright. "Hello, Lily."

Miss Mayfield merely nodded in response, so he filled the conversational void. "I'm doing fine, thank you." He gestured toward her purchase. "That looks like one of Mrs. Mickelson's apple pecan pies. Good choice."

"Momma sent me here to get one for our supper tonight." She tilted her head coquettishly. "We're having a pot roast. You're more than welcome to join us. Mark too, of course."

"That's very generous, but I'll have to decline." He stopped short of coming up with an excuse.

Her lips puckered in a pout, but she recovered quickly. "Perhaps another time."

He dipped his head in a short nod. "If you'll excuse us, Miss Mayfield and I have some things to discuss about the children."

"Of course." She excused herself, and Carson nodded to Miss Mayfield, signaling they should move on.

For a moment neither of them spoke, and then Carson attempted to pick up the conversation where they'd left it. "So what you were saying is that Mark is probably feeling some of this isolation and sense of persecution that you felt."

She shrugged. "I know that everyone doesn't react the same way, and Mark's older than I was at the time, but yes, I acted on that assumption. So first I respected his need to have something that was his alone, that came from his old life and that no one could take from him." Lily again gave that self-deprecating smile. "For me it was singing. My mother loved music, and she used to encourage me and my sister to sing. So whenever I was feeling as if I had nothing of my old life left, I would slip away to somewhere private and just sing out every song I could remember. But I never sang for my grandfather, not in the first year or so anyway."

Is that what Mark thought—that he was trying to erase everything from his old life? "What you're saying is that's why he's always drawing in that notebook of his—it's the only thing he has left from his old life."

She nodded.

He rubbed his chin. "You said not in the first year or so. Does that mean you eventually came around?"

Again she nodded and tucked a stray tendril behind her ear. "It happened for me when I caught my grandfather holding a picture of my mother and he was crying. That's when it hit me that he missed her too. When he spotted me, he waved me over and started talking about her, telling me stories about her as a little girl." Lily was staring straight ahead as she spoke. "Being able to talk about my mother to someone who knew her and loved her too was very healing."

"Unfortunately, Mark doesn't have anyone like that here."

She frowned, her eyes taking on a puzzled look. "I thought I heard you knew his father."

Carson tugged at his cuff, choosing his words carefully. "Mark was barely two when his father died, so he doesn't really remember him. It's his mother he misses, and I didn't know her."

"Oh."

Time to redirect the conversation. "I still don't understand how you took all this experience and got him to interact with you."

"I didn't really do much. I just let him know I understood he wanted to keep his artwork to himself for now and that that was okay. Then I got a little sneaky and asked for his help in a way I knew he wouldn't refuse."

There was a touch of the old Lily in the mischievous grin that accompanied that last sentence.

"Once I had him helping me, I made sure to refer to him often and try to find ways for him to communicate with the other children. I also asked his opinion on a design for the program handbill."

"Handbill?"

The look she turned his way was a little too innocent. "Yes. We need one for the celebration, don't you think?"

He rubbed his jaw. "I suppose it would be a good memento from the celebration."

"Exactly!"

They'd reached the churchyard by this time. He motioned that they should cross the street, and he took her left elbow protectively to help her. With the increasing number of motor cars competing for road usage, one couldn't be too careful.

But at his touch she stiffened and froze for a heartbeat. Her gaze shot to his, and he saw her eyes had widened in surprise.

He raised a brow at her reaction, but he'd felt it too, that little unexpected snap of connection. With a slight touch of pink in her cheeks, she nodded and looked straight ahead as they stepped from the sidewalk.

6

As soon as they'd made it across the street, Carson released her arm and they turned back in the direction they'd come. He kept his own gaze focused straight ahead though he peripherally noted she was doing the same. Just as things threatened to turn awkward, he spotted a member of his congregation approaching and paused. "Mrs. Danner, good day. How's Millard doing?"

"He's doing better, thank you, Pastor." She turned to his companion as if wanting to change the subject. "Hello, Lily. I heard about your arm. I hope it isn't paining you very much."

"It's healing nicely, thank you."

Carson could see the worry beneath Mrs. Danner's outwardly calm appearance. "When will Millard be able to go back to work?"

Her lips compressed and he saw her hands tighten on her bag. "Dr. Martin thinks it may take up to a month for him to be able to get around on his own again."

"I'm so sorry to hear that." He knew the Danvers had already been facing hard times before Millard's accident. "This may not be the best time to bring this up, but I was wondering if you could help me spread the word about something. Mrs. McHale needs a bit of time off, and I need to find someone to take her place for a couple of weeks."

The woman's head came up. "When would you need this person?"

"Tomorrow if possible. Or as soon thereafter as they can."

"I could start tomorrow."

"You? Why that would be excellent. If you're available, why don't you stop by later this afternoon and speak to Mrs. McHale about what all she does." That would hopefully give him time to get to his housekeeper first and let her know she would be taking some time off.

When the woman continued on her way, he was pleased to see she moved with a lighter step.

"That was very kind."

The softly uttered words brought his attention back to his companion. He rubbed the back of his neck. "I had a need I knew she could help me with. That's all it was." Then he quickly brought the conversation back around to their prior topic. "So who will be responsible for this handbill?"

"If you like, I can work with Mark on it since I'm the one who had the idea. We'll want you to approve whatever we come up with, of course." She cut him a challenging glance. "But if you'd prefer to work on it yourself…"

He lifted his palms. "No, I trust you to do a good job of it. And you seem to be on your way to earning Mark's trust."

She nodded but fiddled with her collar, her expression pensive. "Did that answer your questions?"

"Yes. And I appreciate your perspective on this, you've given me a lot to think about." She still had that contemplative air about her. "Was there something else you wanted to discuss?"

She didn't answer for a moment, then gave a small nod as

if she'd made up her mind about something. "I came up with an idea last night that I wanted to go over with you."

"I'm all ears."

"There must be other kids in town besides Mark who either can't or don't want to participate in the play or choir."

"Of course." Why did that sound like a question?

"Then if you have no objections to adding another program to the celebration, I think I have a way to include more of the children and in a way that won't subject them to stage fright and won't take up the time that our practice sessions have." She cut him a sideways glance. "What do you think about a children's art show?"

"Art show?" She'd surprised him yet again. "Did you come up with this idea just to find a way for Mark to participate?" In all good conscience, could he support a program designed just to make Mark feel included?

But she was shaking her head. "I'll admit Mark's interest in drawing is what gave me the idea. This would give him a way to be part of the celebration. But if we did this, we'd be providing an opportunity for all the children, a way to include those who aren't already participating for whatever reason. We could let as many as want to submit a drawing."

Carson tried to look at the idea objectively. "It's an interesting idea. But I'm not sure it's realistic." He gave her an apologetic smile. "It's less than three weeks until the celebration—that doesn't give us much time to plan out and organize a new program, especially when we've never done this sort of thing before."

"Actually, I think that's plenty of time. I can come up with the guidelines, and we can pass the word to all the families in town. In fact, you could announce it from the pulpit on Sunday. And I'm sure two weeks or so is enough time for the children to produce a drawing—it's not as if they'll be doing oil paintings." Before he could respond, she continued. "It wouldn't be a contest, so no judges would be needed—it would just be a way to display the kids' artwork."

"There's still the matter of finding someone to oversee it."

"Actually I was thinking you could do it."

Surely she didn't mean that? "Why me? I don't know much about creating artwork. And not to complain but I already have a lot to do, both for the celebration and for the congregation."

Lily met his gaze with a direct one of her own. "I understand, and if you truly feel that way, I suppose I could do it. After all, I don't think it would take up too much time, and I'm not much use to Aunt Adeline as long as my arm is in a sling."

That made perfect sense to him.

She fingered her collar. "But I thought you might actually *want* to do this." The expression on her face was that of a teacher trying to coax a child to reach the correct solution himself.

"Why?"

"It would give you the chance to work with Mark on something he already enjoys, on a project where he's the expert rather than you. You *are* looking for a way to get closer to him, aren't you?"

She was certainly persuasive. "Yes, of course. But I'm just not sure I have the time—"

The stubborn set of her chin told him she wasn't convinced. "As I said, it shouldn't take much time. You would just need to get the kids who are interested together to discuss the what, where, and when of things and let them know you'll be available to help if needed. Then you can turn them loose to draw. I can help you if you like, but I think you should take the lead."

It was the hopeful way she was looking at him that did him in. He suddenly didn't want to disappoint her. "I suppose I can give it a try." He was rewarded with a sweet smile of approval.

"Good. I think you'll be glad you did in the long run."

"I may need some assistance in creating those guidelines you mentioned."

"I'll give some thought to it this evening and bring my ideas tomorrow when I join you at practice."

Carson nodded.

Her face was alight with her enthusiasm. "We can come up with a theme of sorts—maybe the church itself, or the town—I don't know, but we could come up with something. And then the day of the celebration put all the drawings on display for everyone to enjoy."

She lifted her chin. "But the important thing is that you be the one to tell Mark, and then you try to draw him out."

He wished he could share her certainty that this would help his relationship with Mark. "Easier said than done."

"Not at all. Try to get his suggestions for what materials we'll need, a possible theme, the best way to display the finished pieces—those sorts of things." She gave him another of those pointed looks. "The thing to remember is that while you two are discussing all of this that you really listen and let him know you respect his ideas."

"I can do that." He smiled. "In case I haven't said it already, I'm very grateful you made this effort for Mark." Though he wasn't sure if his relationship with the boy would ever get past the polite stage.

Lily seemed to know what he was thinking. She reached out and touched his sleeve briefly. "Don't worry, I have faith that he'll come around eventually."

Have faith—a good reminder. Carson straightened. "We should bring this up to the committee this afternoon."

"Committee?"

Had she hit her head when she fell and injured her arm? "Yes. Don't tell me you've forgotten the entire anniversary celebration committee meets at two o'clock this afternoon."

Her cheeks pinkened. "Actually I'm afraid I had. But yes,

we can bring it up to them. You don't think anyone will object do you?"

"Not at all. This is just to keep everyone informed. Since you and I are in charge of the children's part of the program, there's no reason for them to object."

They'd reached the spot directly across from Adeline's Fashion Emporium. This time he extended his bent arm and allowed her to hold on to him as they crossed the street. Once on the sidewalk in front of the shop, he gave her a short bow. "I'll leave you here. Thank you for taking the time to speak to me this morning."

"You're quite welcome. I enjoyed it." Her cheeks turned that becoming shade of pink again. "The chance to get out and walk on such a fine day I mean." And with that she quickly turned and entered the dress shop.

VIOLET ENTERED THE DRESS SHOP, feeling energized by her discussion with the pastor. Everything she'd done since trading places with Lily to this point had been done with the intention of not straying from the way her sister did things. Working on the flyer with Mark and helping the pastor with the art show gave her more freedom to just be herself. Of course she'd still need to keep up the pretense of being Lily, but she could do so while not worrying about what had already been said or done because she was starting from scratch.

And her mind was already bubbling with ideas she could discuss with the pastor tomorrow.

The pastor.

Her mood shifted. When he'd taken her arm, she'd felt something, something unexpected that didn't bear close scrutiny. He'd noticed, naturally—the man didn't seem to miss much. She'd just reacted out of surprise, of course. Growing up on the ranch and then moving into the small, closed community of the circus, she wasn't used to such considerations.

But it was more than that. He'd asked for her help and had really listened to her ideas. The approval in his eyes had given her spirits a lift in a way that was quite heady. It was nice to be appreciated for something other than her skill with a gun.

Carson was different from what she expected a pastor to be.

He wasn't sober and dull, he actually had a dry sense of humor. He had yet to connect with Mark, something you'd expect a pastor to be able to do. And rather than have infinite patience, she'd seen frustration cross his expression a time or two when his attempts to reach out to Mark fell flat.

But for all that, he was a good man. He'd seemed genuinely concerned about her when she showed up with her arm in a sling yesterday. It was obvious he was good with the children in the program. He'd been exceedingly kind to Mrs. Danner when he'd encountered her earlier, being careful of her dignity. And he'd handled that flirt from the bakery with tact.

It was easy to see why Lily was so smitten with him. As it was, she was having a difficult time remembering that the pastor thought she was Lily, not Violet. Of course, she'd only met the man yesterday, so it was silly for her to think she'd developed any sort of feelings for him beyond a desire to be friends. And, given his calling, even that would likely be impossible if he found out she was pretending to be someone she wasn't.

Which is why she had to make sure he never found out. Because if he *did* find out, both she and Lily would be painted with the same liar's brush. And she couldn't bear the thought of Lily being hurt because she'd agreed to this swap.

Perhaps she would write her sister a letter this evening.

But what would she say? How deeply do you like Pastor

Carson because I think I might be developing feelings too? That would never do. No, it would be best if she just nipped this in the bud. The pastor was a charming man, and he appreciated her help with the children's program, but that was all.

In the meantime, she'd just focus on the tasks at hand. And first on the list was to question Aunt Adeline about who was on this committee the pastor mentioned and what she should expect to face when they met this afternoon.

"THANK YOU FOR YOUR REPORT, Howard. It sounds like your team has the construction projects well in hand."

Violet sat in the second pew, watching as the pastor ran the committee meeting. So far Margaret Jones had given a report on the refreshment committee and Howard Branch had given his report on the construction committee. It turned out this celebration was a bigger event than Violet had supposed.

She had to admit, Pastor Carson looked very commanding standing in front of the small group, asking questions and keeping everyone focused on the business at hand without being overbearing.

"Miss Kester, do you have an update from the decorating committee for us?"

Violet watched as a young lady about her age stood and moved to the front of the room. "Thank you, Pastor. I'm pleased to report that thanks to some donations by Fuller's Store we were able to gather up all our materials for less than we budgeted." Her tone and expression were triumphant.

After a smattering of applause, the thrifty decorator continued. "Tonight we want to run two options by you for the bunting on the stage and booths."

As Brenda presented the relative merits of cotton versus linen and royal blue versus sky blue, Violet let her thoughts wander. Thanks to what she'd heard from Aunt Adeline, she knew the next report would come from Mrs. Tolby, who was in charge of the lunch basket auction. After that, she and the pastor would report on the children's program and that would close out the meeting.

She was looking forward to the pastor's report on the children's project. It would be interesting to hear how he presented the art show project.

"Miss Mayfield, would you like to come up and report on the children's program?"

That caught Violet by surprise. She'd just assumed the pastor would give the report. But she stood and eased from the pew and moved to the front. It would have been nice to have had some warning. Then again, maybe this was something that would have been automatically assumed by Lily. "I'm pleased to say that both the play and the choir practices are going very well. The children are learning their parts and are really enthusiastic. They seem to be looking forward to performing on stage for the entire congregation."

She glanced toward Pastor Carson, uncertain if he wanted her to present their idea for the art show or if he wanted to do that himself.

Apparently understanding her unspoken question, he jumped in. "Miss Mayfield and I have an addition to the children's program I think you all are going to like. And since it was Miss Mayfield's splendid idea, I'll let her tell you about it."

So he was handing it back over to her. Pasting on a smile, she turned to face the committee. "We're going to invite the children to submit drawings or paintings that we'll display the day of the celebration—an art show of sorts. It'll be open to any child who wants to participate."

"But there's just a little over two weeks left before the celebration." The head of the refreshment committee's lips were pinched. "Why add something this late?"

"As Miss Mayfield accurately pointed out when she discussed the idea with me, there are quite a few children in town who can't or don't feel comfortable participating in the play or choir. This will give them a chance to still have something showcased."

"Will the pictures be judged?"

"No," Pastor Carson explained. "It won't be a competition, just a show."

Brenda Kester spoke up. "Well, I for one think it's a lovely idea. And I'm happy to volunteer to help in any way I can." The smile she gave the pastor was bright enough to light up a cellar. Was this another contender for his favors?

"Thank you, that's very generous." The pastor nodded appreciatively. "But you already have your hands full with the decorating committee. Miss Mayfield and I will be able to handle this."

A flash of vexation was quickly replaced with a breezy smile. "Very well, but don't hesitate to call on me if you should need help."

With a nod, Pastor Carson turned back to the committee. "Now, is there any new business for the group to discuss?" When there was no response, he spread his hands. "Then I think this meeting is adjourned. We'll all meet back here next Wednesday, same time. But if anything comes up between now and then that needs our attention, let me know."

The group stood but didn't immediately move to the door, instead milling about and socializing as if they hadn't seen each other in weeks. Not wanting to get into conversation with these people she supposedly knew well, Violet headed down the aisle, ready to make her escape. But she hadn't made it past the third pew when she was stopped by a hail.

"Miss Mayfield, if you have a moment before you leave…"

She turned to see Pastor Carson heading her way. Over his shoulder she spotted Brenda with an annoyed expression on her face.

Violet stood where she was, letting the pastor come to her.

"You seem to be in a big hurry to leave."

"I've been gone from the dress shop far too much the past few days." She tucked a lock of hair behind her ear. "Was there something you needed from me?"

"I thought you'd like to know that Mrs. McHale happily agreed to take a couple of weeks off and Mrs. Danvers is meeting with her now."

She felt a little flutter of pleasure that he'd wanted to share that with her. "That *is* good news."

He returned her smile. "I also have a favor to ask."

Intriguing. "Of course."

"I plan to visit our congregation's shut-ins on Friday morning. And I find some of the females in these households are more comfortable if I have a lady with me when I visit."

Was he asking her to join him? "Who do you normally bring with you on these visits?"

He gave her a searching look, as if confused by her question. Uh-oh, that meant she probably should have already known.

"Usually Mrs. Stansbury," he finally answered. "But she's unavailable this week."

Who in the world was Mrs. Stansbury? But of course that was something else she should have known, so she couldn't ask.

Because she was so eager to say yes, Violet hesitated. Then she answered with a question of her own. "How long would you need me for?"

"I set out around nine thirty, and it usually takes two to

three hours to make the rounds." His brows drew down in a puzzled expression. "I apologize for putting you on the spot. If you'd rather not—"

Violet quickly pulled herself together. She had to remember to respond as Lily would, which would most likely be a happy yes. "No apologies needed. I'm honored you'd trust me with such a task. I'll just need to discuss my availability with Aunt Adeline."

His expression cleared. "Of course. You can let me know at practice tomorrow."

She cast another quick glance over his shoulder, then met his gaze again. "But if I do have to bow out, I'm sure you won't have trouble finding another lady to join you."

He raised a brow at that and his lips twitched. "Let's hope we won't have to put that to the test."

She grinned at that, then turned and headed for the door, her steps feeling lighter than before.

She tried to convince herself that she was doing this for Lily's sake, that that was what was behind the little bubble of happiness in her chest.

But a small voice told her there was another reason altogether.

7

C arson sat in his study, staring at the night sky outside his window, reflecting on his day.

Mrs. McHale had departed for the evening—but not before telling him she'd made sure he'd be in good hands with Janet Danvers—and Mark was in bed, so the house was quiet.

The discussion with Lily had been enlightening in more than one way. As he'd hoped, it had given him insights into how to try to draw Mark out of his shell. But it had also given him a deeper understanding of who she was. It was a testament to God's providence that she'd grown into a woman with such a sunny, positive disposition. Though the past few days he'd seen a quieter, more vulnerable side of her. And one with more ingenuity. Truth to tell, seeing this side of Lily intrigued him, made him want to learn more.

Resolutely pushing those thoughts aside, Carson turned them instead to Mark. After the committee meeting, he'd talked to the boy about the planned art show. There'd been a flash of interest in Mark's expression, but it had quickly disappeared behind a suspicious watchfulness. Carson wasn't sure if that was a step up from indifference or not.

But he'd pressed on, trying to draw him into a discussion of themes and supplies and the best way to organize everything, but Mark hadn't contributed much. Carson had finally given up and just asked him to give it some thought.

It seemed Miss Mayfield had been overly optimistic in her thoughts on how this would draw him and Mark together.

Or maybe it was just him. Did he not have it in him to be a father? What did it say about his ability to be a pastor?

"So who'd like to go first?"

Carson leaned back in his chair. He, Lily, and Mark had headed for the church office as soon as the children's practice ended.

Lily dug a notebook out of her bag. "I'll start if you like. I wrote down a few thoughts last night that I can share with you."

Carson smiled at her obvious enthusiasm.

"For a theme," she continued, "I'm thinking we open it up to anything that touches on the anniversary itself. That gives lots of freedom to our young artists. What do you gentlemen think?"

Carson nodded. "That makes sense."

She turned to Mark. "What do you think?"

The boy traced the edge of his notebook with a finger. "I suppose that would work."

Her brow drew down in question. "But there's something about it you don't like."

His head came up and his eyes widened, as if surprised she'd noticed. "I didn't say that."

But she didn't let it go at that. "Please. I want to hear your thoughts. You have more experience than either me or Pastor Carson with what an artist needs in the way of direction."

There was an earnestness in Lily's question, a respect in the way she looked at the boy, as if she were discussing this with a peer.

And Mark responded by sitting up a bit straighter and meeting her gaze. "I think you should be more specific."

Specific? That was an interesting word choice for a nine-year-old.

Lily, however, was focusing on his statement. "Isn't keeping it open to whatever the person wants to draw a good thing?"

Mark looked down again, but Carson didn't sense a withdrawal this time. Rather, the boy's mood seemed pensive. "I was just thinking about something my momma used to say. On Sundays, when the weather was nice, we'd go on picnics and she'd ask me to draw something for her."

Carson went still and stared at the boy's bent head. It was the first time he'd heard Mark speak of his mother since the woman's funeral.

"At first I'd just do sketches of the meadows and fields where we had the picnics. But then Momma asked me to be more specific. She said the other pictures were nice but there was more truth in a picture of a single flower or insect or bird than in a landscape that has no focus. And that a person should always strive for truth."

Lily's expression softened. "Your mother must have been a wonderful person."

Mark nodded but didn't look up.

"Well, I think you're right." Her voice had a bracing quality to it. "We *should* be more specific. Do you have any ideas on what the focus should be?"

Mark seemed to think about that a moment. Then he met

her gaze. "The celebration is about the church, so I think that should be the focus."

Carson decided to join the conversation. "You mean the church building itself?"

Mark nodded. "Yes, but not just that. It could be the entire building or just the front door or the steeple or those rose vines climbing up the wall by the side entrance. Or it could be the inside of the church, focusing on the pews or the organ or the pulpit." He waved a hand. "Or anything else having to do with the church. That way it gives everyone the freedom to pick from lots of different views, but it's also more focused."

Lily nodded. "So that's where the choice and imagination come in."

"It sounds like we have our theme." Carson was sure to include Mark in his praise. "Good job."

Then he smiled Lily's way. "What's next? I'm sure there's more in that notebook of yours."

She sat up straighter, her eyes alight with enthusiasm. "Yes. I also made a checklist of the things we'll need to do to make this project a success. I thought the three of us could go over it and see what I left off and then decide which one of us will be in charge of getting what done."

And just like that she'd woven in another thread to make Mark feel included. How did she make it seem so effortless? "Let's hear it."

She read through her list, and he and Mark gave some input. Then she sat back. "I think we have a pretty good list here. And it all seems doable in the time we have left before the celebration."

"I agree." Carson laced his fingers on his desk. "All we need to do now is get enough of the children interested to have a good showing." He turned to Mark. "You do plan to participate, don't you?"

But the boy merely shrugged.

Would Mark have answered differently if Lily had asked the question? Carson fought to keep the disappointment out of his voice. "I must say, I expected you to be a little more excited about the event."

Mark's expression twisted into resentment. "Don't you think I know what you're doing? You came up with this idea at the last minute just because you want me to be part of this celebration. Because it won't look good if the pastor's kid doesn't participate."

Did the boy think so little of him? "That's not it at all." He leaned forward, trying to convey his sincerity. "Yes, the fact that you like to draw is what gave Miss Mayfield the idea, but I didn't agree to it just because I was trying to avoid embarrassment. It was because I'd like you and any other child who can't take part in the other programs to have something they'd enjoy doing."

Mark didn't look entirely convinced, but the distrust in his expression had dimmed a bit.

Lily placed a hand lightly on the boy's knee. "And I was hoping you could actually help us out since neither of us have any experience in this area." She leaned back and waved a hand. "Maybe answer questions or give quick lessons for those less experienced than you. And if you really don't want to provide an actual drawing for the show, that's entirely your choice."

Mark shifted in his chair, his uncertainty obvious.

"What about it? Miss Mayfield and I have our hands full with the play and choir groups. Will you at least help us keep things organized and let us know when our assistance is needed?"

"It would truly be a big help."

The boy sat up straighter. "All right. I can do that."

"Excellent." Carson decided to be thankful for any sign of

progress, no matter how small. "We can have the children work here when the other practice is going on or work at home if they can't be here."

"That sounds like a good plan." Lily stood. "Now, if you gentlemen will excuse me, I need to get back to the dress shop."

"Of course." As Carson stood, he was pleased to see Mark do the same.

"If you'll wait here," he said to the boy, "I want to escort Miss Mayfield out."

Mark nodded and pulled out his notebook and pencil as Carson opened the door.

LILY WALKED beside the pastor as they made their way from the church office to the auditorium. She should have told him to stay behind with Mark, that she was perfectly capable of seeing herself out, but she hadn't quite been able to get the words out.

He spoke first. "How do you feel about how things went?"

A nice safe topic. "I was certainly hoping Mark would participate in the show itself." She sent him a bracing smile. "But he did agree to help us out. And you have to admit, if he's only willing to do one or the other, that's the one you want."

"You're right I suppose." He rubbed his jaw. "At least he took an active part in the conversation. I think he said more to me just now and showed more emotion than any other time since he's been here."

He seemed to need some encouragement. "And now that you've taken that first step, I think it'll be easier to build on it."

"I hope you're right."

"I am." She met his gaze. "You just need to have faith."

He grimaced good-naturedly. "You're right—I shouldn't need to be reminded of that."

"By the way, I noticed Joey did much better at practice today."

"He did." The pastor gave her a smile. "Thanks to your suggestion on script changes."

They'd reached the exit by then, and he changed the subject before she could respond. "Are you going to do a basket for the auction this year? Or will having only one hand to work with make it too difficult?"

Basket? Did he mean one of those lunch auction baskets the committee had reported on yesterday? She should have paid better attention. "I haven't decided yet," she said carefully.

"Well, if you decide to prepare something, regardless of the outcome, I imagine there are any number of young men who'd be willing to bid on it just for the pleasure of your company."

That sounded intriguing. But of course he meant for the pleasure of Lily's company, not hers. He opened the door for her, and she made her exit.

As she descended the steps to the churchyard, she thought about the letter to Lily she'd posted this morning. She'd told her sister all that had gone on since they'd swapped places and asked for a similar report from her. How was her stylish townie of a sister doing in the rough world of a traveling circus? Was she regretting having agreed to the swap yet, or was she enjoying the change of surroundings and expectations the way she herself was?

She'd also done her best to ask questions that would help her figure out just how interested Lily was in the pastor. For some reason, that had become important for her to know.

Later, at the Emporium, when there were no customers around, Violet brought up her conversation with Carson. "The pastor asked me about preparing a basket for the celebration. Do you know what he was talking about?"

Her aunt's brow went up. "He asked you about that?" Then she turned back to the dress she was fitting to a dress form for display. "One of the things we traditionally do on the celebration day is have a lunch basket auction. The ladies prepare a picnic lunch, and the men bid on a basket of their choosing. Along with the basket comes the honor of sharing it with the lady who prepared it. The baskets are submitted anonymously, so supposedly the men don't know whose basket they are bidding on." She grinned. "It's old-fashioned, but it makes for great fun to see who gets paired up, even if it's just for a meal."

Violet's mind went immediately to figuring out what she could prepare one-handed. Then her head came up. "Wait, you said supposedly."

Adeline chuckled. "There's more than one young lady who'll let her beau—or someone she hopes will become her beau—know what kind of ribbon or cover cloth is on her basket."

Violet shared her aunt's grin. "And Lily participated?"

"She did. After all, the money earned goes to the upkeep of the church building and grounds." Her aunt waved a hand. "And Lily never let a little thing like not being a good cook stop her." Then she glanced over her shoulder at Violet. "Are you thinking about preparing a basket?"

"I should, don't you think? I mean it's what Lily would be expected to do." Surely that was her only reason for feeling so eager about it.

"You could quite legitimately use your injury as an excuse not to."

Was her aunt trying to talk her out of it? "We'll see. I can wait until it's closer to time to decide."

"Of course."

There was something in her aunt's tone she couldn't quite identify. But rather than digging deeper, she tried another question. "Is there anyone in particular who would be interested in bidding on Lily's basket?"

"Do you mean does she have any admirers?" The older woman shrugged. "There are one or two young men in town who have shown an interest, but she hasn't encouraged any of them."

Violet nodded. "Because she has her heart set on Pastor Carson."

"Because your sister needs a challenge." Her aunt's tone was dry. "She doesn't want a man who'll come running every time she crooks her finger."

Was that why Lily had developed an interest in the pastor, because he was a challenge? Definitely something to think about. But right now it was time to turn the tables. "Are you going to make a basket?"

Aunt Adeline chuckled. "I don't think anyone would be looking forward to sharing a basket with me."

"Why not? I can vouch for how delicious your meals are."

"There's usually a flirtatious component to these things, at least for the single folks. Or for the married couples for that matter—husbands will bid on their wives' baskets."

Violet wasn't going to let her get away with that. "I do believe there may be a certain gentleman here in town who would be very interested in your basket in particular."

Her aunt's cheeks pinkened, and she kept her gaze focused on the garment as she spoke. "I have no idea what you're talking about. However, the proceeds do go to a good cause, so I suppose it makes sense that the more baskets the better." Then she pointed to a nearby display. "Hand me that green ribbon please."

Violet handed her aunt the requested ribbon. "Now tell me what else happens at this church anniversary celebration so I'll be better prepared the next time I get asked a question like that."

Before the seamstress could respond, the shop door opened, signaling they were no longer alone. As soon as she recognized who'd walked in, Violet straightened and tucked a lock of hair behind her ear.

8

C arson stepped into the Fashion Emporium for the second time in as many days. Mark was with him and looked decidedly uncomfortable in this feminine establishment.

Lily stepped forward. "Is there something I can help you with?"

"Mark and I are going to Fuller's Store to shop for the art supplies we'll need. I thought you might want to join us."

Lily didn't answer right away. Instead, she glanced toward her aunt. The woman nodded and made a shooing hand gesture in response. "Go on. I have two fittings this afternoon, but they're not for another hour. I can take care of any walk-ins until then."

Lily turned to face him. "It looks like I'm available."

As they walked the short distance to their destination, Lily did her best to engage Mark in discussion, meeting with mixed success. Carson held his peace, deciding she was better at this than he was.

When they arrived at the three-story redbrick structure that housed Fuller's, Carson grabbed a shopping basket for himself and handed one to Mark. Then he led them directly to the area where the art supplies were displayed.

"Do you have any guess of how many children should we expect to participate?" Lily asked.

"Hard to say since we've never done anything like this before." Carson tugged the cuff of his shirt. "I think we can start by getting enough materials for about a dozen young artists. If more decide to join, we can always buy additional supplies."

"That sounds like a good plan." Lily turned to Mark. "What do you suggest we get?"

Mark studied the art supplies with a clear-to-see longing. "I suppose pencils and those large drawing pads."

Carson loaded the named items in his basket. Then he noted Mark's gaze was focused on the crayons and paints.

"I think we can do better than this." Carson gathered up several boxes of wax crayons and colored pencils and dropped them in Mark's basket. Then he added pens and ink to his own. He glanced at Mark, whose eyes had grown wide. "Should I add charcoals?"

Mark seemed to think about it a moment, and Carson could see he was tempted, but he finally shook his head. "I think we can do everything we need to with these."

Carson resisted the urge to get them anyway. Lily had said to let Mark know that his input was respected.

Before they could move on, Lily spoke up. "If it'll fit within our budget, why don't we get that stack of poster boards too? We can use them to attach the finished pieces to. It'll give them a more uniform look."

"Good idea." Carson was feeling expansive. The boy had asked for so little since he'd been in Larkin that he would gladly add a little of his own money to the mix.

Lily held out her free arm. "Let me have your basket so you can carry those more comfortably."

At his raised brow, she rolled her eyes and jutted her chin. "Just because I have one arm in a sling doesn't mean I'm helpless."

Deciding to give in with good grace, he handed over his basket and picked up the stack of poster boards. "I think that's everything."

A few minutes later they were at the register where Patience Anderson greeted them. "Goodness, Pastor, it looks like you're going to be starting an art school down at the church."

"Actually we're adding a children's art show to the church anniversary celebration. If your Minnie and Dennis would like to take part, they're quite welcome to."

Patience smiled. "Thank you. I'll let them know."

"And tell them to spread the word," Lily added. "The more participants we have the better."

Once they were out on the sidewalk again, Lily turned to Mark. "So have you changed your mind about taking part? It would be a shame to put all this work into getting everything organized and not enjoy the fun of actually doing the artwork."

Mark merely shrugged.

But Lily seemed determined to engage the boy. "Well, if you did decide to take part, which of the drawing mediums would you want to use?"

This time Mark spoke up quickly. "The colored pencils."

Carson hid a smile. She'd managed to draw him out after all.

"And what would you draw?" Her tone was casual, as if she and Mark were in the middle of a friendly discussion.

"The front of the church."

He'd obviously already given this some thought. "Why that particular image?" Carson hoped he wouldn't set Mark's back up by joining the conversation.

"Because the carvings on the door and the shape of the porch roof are interesting, especially when taken together."

"I guess I never noticed that before. You definitely have an artist's eye."

Apparently he'd said the right thing because Mark stood a bit taller all of a sudden. Perhaps he could try something new. "What do you think Mark, should we treat Miss Mayfield to a cinnamon sugar cookie from Mickelson's Bakery before we deliver her back to the dress shop?"

Mark nodded an enthusiastic agreement.

"I accept your most gracious offer," Lily said with mock formality.

"Then it's agreed. A stop at the bakery it is."

Mark walked slightly ahead of the adults, leading the way.

After a few seconds of silence, Lily spoke up. "So what do you do on the shut-in visits?"

He smiled. "For the most part I just sit and converse with them. I'll pray with them, listen to them, and just in general be good company."

She imagined his presence brought peace and comfort to the lonely and hurting. "And what is it you need me to do?"

"Having a female presence is the main thing. But at some point during each visit I'll need you to find a reason to excuse yourself so if there's something personal they wish to discuss with a pastor, they can do so."

"I understand."

They'd reached the bakery, and Mark was waiting for them, his eyes focused on a boy using a short length of rope to play tug-of-war with a dog. There was something in the boy's expression Violet couldn't quite read.

"Ready for that cookie?"

The pastor's question brought Mark back to the present, and whatever that expression had meant, it was gone, replaced by eager anticipation for the promised treat.

Fifteen minutes later, Violet entered the dress shop with a smile on her face. She'd enjoyed the time spent with Mark and the pastor. And the way Mark's defenses were beginning to give way was a big part of it.

It had been so satisfying to see the beginning of a connection between the pastor and the boy and to know she'd played some small part in that.

Truth to tell, knowing the pastor had gone out of his way to ask her to take part in this shopping trip and to accompany him for the shut-in visitation tomorrow made her feel special, sought after, which was a new experience for her. And it was a feeling she liked.

Until she remembered it was Lily he'd sought out, not her.

CARSON WAS DEFINITELY ENCOURAGED. Mark was finally coming out from behind those walls he'd erected.

As Lily had predicted, this art show idea had given him and Mark something to not only discuss but work on together. Even if Mark wasn't quite ready to fully trust him, Carson could now see a way forward for them.

Lily had not only shared her own experiences, painful as that must have been, but she had used them to provide some important insights to help him understand what might be going on in Mark's head. And it had shifted his whole perception of the boy's needs and character, had changed how he tried to interact with him.

For that he would be forever in Lily's debt.

Lily.

He was ashamed to say that there was so much more to her

than he'd given her credit for. It sounded as if she'd experienced a very painful and lonely childhood. Not that he'd sensed any conscious fishing for sympathy in her story. God be praised that she'd turned into such an optimistic, caring person.

It was like he hadn't really seen her, the true her, until she'd hurt her wrist. Was it because the accident had made her feel more vulnerable and open to others? Or was the change inside himself because of the prayer he'd voiced there in the garden and the vow to be open to finding a wife?

Either way, he was seeing her now.

"Are you sure you don't want me to carry that for you?" It was Friday morning and Carson had stopped by the dress shop to collect Lily. Now the two of them were walking down the sidewalk and turning toward the more residential part of town. Lily carried a cloth-covered basket on her good arm.

"I'm sure."

He'd been waiting for her to tell him why she'd brought a cloth-covered basket with her, but his curiosity finally got the better of him. "If you don't mind my asking, what's in it?"

"Cookies," she said proudly. "I had Aunt Adeline help me bake them last night." She ducked her head with a self-deprecating smile. "I thought it would be nice to have a little something to give the people we visit. I hope that's okay."

"It's more than okay. It's very thoughtful." That shy, vulnerable smile touched him every time.

Her cheeks pinkened and her smile widened as if he'd just given her a gift. But all she said was "So where are we headed?"

"I thought we'd start with the shut-ins here in town. We won't need to spend as much time with them as those who are out of town because they live closer to their neighbors and have more people drop in to check on them."

She nodded. "That makes sense. How many homes are we going to visit?"

"Three here in town. We'll start with the Mercers. Michael is still recovering from his fractured foot, and Loretta came down with a cough this week."

"I'll admit to being a little nervous."

"Why? You know the Mercers. They're both very nice, even-tempered people."

Her eyes widened, then her lips twisted in a wince. But her expression cleared quickly. "You're right. It's just, well, this somehow feels different, more formal."

Another of those unexpected reactions that seemed out of place. Was it possible Lily had hit her head when she hurt her arm? But he needed to respond to her concerns. "Once we get started, those jitters will go away."

Lily lifted her chin with a breezy smile that was reminiscent of the old Lily. "I'm sure you're right."

A few moments later they reached the Mercers' place. To his surprise she nearly walked right past their front gate. "We're here," he prompted.

Chagrin flashed in her expression, then she gave a self-deprecating grimace. "Sorry, I guess I let my mind wander." And with a slight toss of her head, she preceded him through the gate he held open.

It turned out her cookies were a big hit. The Mercers made much over her offering and proclaimed them to be delicious.

Lily didn't try to take the lead in the discussion but contributed in a way that helped draw the older couple out. Then, during a conversational pause ten minutes into their visit, she stood and smiled. "I noticed your beautiful roses when we came in. Would you mind if I took a closer look at them?"

So she'd remembered to give him time alone with the homeowners.

Mrs. Mercer grabbed for her cane, but Lily waved her back down. "There's no need for you to trouble yourself. I won't be long."

The woman nodded through another coughing fit and settled back down.

VIOLET MADE it through the first two visits without anyone suspecting she wasn't Lily, and she started to relax. As long as she let Carson take the lead on the conversations, she could figure enough out through context to keep people from looking at her responses too closely.

As they left Mr. Folse's home, she cut Carson a sideways look. "What's our next stop?"

"The Baylor sisters' home. I don't know if you've heard, but Miss Louann took sick on Wednesday. To be honest, I think she's been pouring everything she has into taking care of Miss Georgia for so long that she's just exhausted."

What was wrong that this Miss Georgia needed someone to care for her full time? "So who's taking care of Miss Georgia while her sister is ill?"

His brow furrowed as he gave her a why-are-you-asking look. "Miss Della, of course."

"Oh yes, of course." It was obvious from the look he was giving her that she should have known that. And just when she was congratulating herself for how well she was doing.

Luckily they arrived at their destination before he could probe further.

Carson's knock was answered by a spare gray-haired woman in an outdated dress, who looked to be in her fifties. "Pastor, Lily, what a pleasant surprise. Please come in."

"Thank you, Miss Della. We promise not to stay long."

Thank goodness the pastor had used her name.

"You can stay just as long as you like, Pastor Davis."

Was there a touch of flirtation in the woman's voice? If Carson heard it, he didn't let on.

Violet found the three sisters absolutely delightful—eccentric but delightful. They all flirted outrageously with Pastor Carson, Miss Louann insisted on showing them her button collection, and Miss Georgia, who was wheelchair bound, read them some of the poetry she'd written.

After the second poem, a multi-stanza tribute to their pet cat Buttermilk, the pastor stood. "If you ladies don't mind, I noticed one of the spindles on the porch rail was loose. I'd like to see if I can tighten it or if I should send someone to fix it for you."

"That's quite generous of you, Pastor Davis." Della stood. "I'll go with you in case you need anything."

"Thank you, but that's not really necessary. I—"

"Nonsense. I don't mind." And without waiting for his response, she breezed from the room.

Violet tried to hide her amusement, but when Carson cast her a helpless look, she almost laughed out loud. Instead, she turned and engaged the remaining women in conversation.

Once he'd made his exit, Violet turned to the remaining sister. "This tea is delicious, Miss Louann. Do you have a secret?"

The woman preened. "I add just a pinch of cinnamon. It gives it a nice sassy note don't you think?" Then she frowned. "But I thought I'd told you that once before."

Violet took a sip from her cup to give herself time to think.

Luckily Georgia intervened. "Don't quiz the girl, sister. I'm sure her injury this week has her rattled."

That didn't make sense, but the sisters seemed to take it as a reasonable explanation, so Violet pressed on. "Is there anything I can do for either of you? Anything at all?"

"That's very sweet of you. I could use another skein of dark green embroidery thread if you would be so kind as to pick some up for me."

"Of course." She turned to Miss Georgia. "How about you? I see from the bookmark peeking out of your book that you're nearly done. Would you like me to stop by the library and pick up a new book for you?" She'd seen the town library on her walks to the church.

"Oh, that would be lovely, dear. Just tell Eugenia it's for me—she knows what kind of books I like."

"I'll stop by the library tomorrow."

They chatted a bit longer, discussing everything from teacups to doilies, and the ladies seemed very disappointed that she had no gossip to share.

Finally Violet stood. "I've enjoyed the visit, but I should be going." She gathered up her basket. "Pastor Carson and I have a few more stops to make today."

When Violet stepped outside, she saw Miss Della sitting on the porch swing, chatting happily to the pastor about what a good year this was for blackberries.

The pastor stood and bowed slightly to his companion. "I believe the porch rail is secure now. If you'll excuse us, Miss Mayfield and I should be on our way."

The woman gave a little pout. "If you must go, then I suppose you must. But please come back soon."

He smiled and merely said, "I hope to see you in church on Sunday." Then he escorted Violet down the stairs.

Violet waited until they turned on the sidewalk to say anything. Then she gave him a sideways look. "It was nice of Miss Della to keep you company."

He lifted his head and gave her a stern look. "Miss Della is a very friendly woman."

"I saw that." She waited a heartbeat, then added, "Very friendly."

His expression cracked and he grinned. "No one could ever accuse Miss Della of being subtle." Then he changed the subject. "The rest of our visits are too far to walk. I hope you don't mind that I hired a buggy instead of a motorcar."

Violet had never ridden in a motorcar before. Had Lily? But she merely nodded.

Fifteen minutes later they were seated in a buggy headed out of town.

"What's our next stop?"

"Elmer Voorhes's place."

"He's been ill?"

"Not exactly. Ever since Hazel passed last month, he's been having trouble adjusting. You may have noticed he hasn't been back to church service." The pastor rubbed the back of his neck. "His sister moved in to help him, of course, but it's not the same."

"Of course it's not. It must be so difficult to go through something like the loss of a spouse. I can't imagine the heartache." Then she remembered he was a widower. She shot him a horrified look in time to see his jaw tighten.

How could she have been so thoughtless?

9

"Oh, I'm sorry. I didn't mean—"

Carson heard the sincere regret in her voice and tried to ease her worry. "It's all right. It's been two years since my wife passed."

She was quiet for a moment, then she cut him a sideways glance. "Do you mind if I ask how she died?" Then she hurriedly added, "But don't feel you have to. I'm sorry, that was terribly—"

"A fever took her," he said abruptly, halting her protest. "It happened very quickly. I'd gone to a conference two states away, so I wasn't home when she took to her bed. They sent me word, but by the time I made it back, it was already too late." That had been a difficult time for him. He'd felt guilty on several levels, including guilt over his feelings of relief.

Ready to change the subject, he pointed out a hawk circling overhead, and the conversation settled into safer, less personal topics the rest of the way to Elmer's.

The visit with the widowed horse rancher passed quickly. The man's head injury was nearly healed, and after a bit of prodding, he promised he would go to town at least twice a week—once to take his sister to do her shopping and run errands and on Sundays to attend church service.

As Carson was helping Violet into the buggy, something tumbled from her pocket. Once he was sure she was settled, he stooped down to retrieve it. It turned out to be a colorful stone that was polished as if it had come from a riverbed. He held it out to her on his open palm. "Did you drop this?"

Her eyes widened and she flashed a grateful smile as she snatched it from him. "Oh goodness yes. Thank you so much. I couldn't bear it if I lost this."

There had to be a story there. He walked around and climbed up in the buggy and took the reins. "So what's so special about that bit of rock?"

"It's what it represents." She was quiet a moment as she rubbed the stone with her thumb. "I found this at the edge of a creek when I was five years old. My parents had taken me and my sister on a picnic. It was a glorious spring day. The weather was perfect, wildflowers were everywhere, and my sister and I chased butterflies and dragonflies. The four of us picked dewberries and ate them straight from the vine. I can still remember how they exploded in my mouth with juicy pops. It was as if God had said here, this is my gift to you."

He could tell she was no longer with him here in the buggy but back in that meadow on that long ago day.

"Anyway, we were walking along the creek bank, looking at tadpoles and minnows, when I spotted the prettiest stone I ever did see. Daddy looked at it and said I had a keen eye and I should hold it, stare at it, and think about all the fun we'd had that day. And then every time I looked at it in the future, I'd remember just how good it felt."

"Sounds as if your father was an interesting man."

She nodded and swallowed hard, her expression somber. "Two days later my parents were in the accident that killed them. But I always remembered what he said about this rock.

Holding it and remembering that one perfect day got me through some really difficult times."

No wonder that bit of stone meant so much to her. Before he could come up with something appropriate to say, she cleared her throat. "Where are we headed now?"

He accepted her change of subject. "Our last stop is Vera Franklin's place. According to Emma, Vera took sick earlier this week. Emma's been looking in on her, but I'm sure with six kids and an orchard to manage, Vera could use a bit of extra encouragement."

"Vera's lucky to have someone like Emma to look in on her."

There was something almost tentative about her tone. "Well, yes. Being sisters and both widows I suppose they feel a special bond."

"Of course." Then she straightened and lifted the cover of her basket.

"Is something wrong?"

She shook her head. "I just wanted to make sure I have enough cookies left for all six kids." She flashed him a bright smile. "And I do."

"That's good," he said as he turned the buggy onto a drive, "because here we are."

As with everyone else she'd given them to, Lily's cookies were a big hit with the children.

Vera smiled as Lily handed them the basket and told them they could have all that were left. "That's very kind of you. They haven't had many treats lately."

"I'm just happy to have someone to bake for. I don't get much chance to do much of that since"—Lily's cheeks pinkened—"well, since I started helping with the children's program."

He could tell she hadn't meant to say that. Was her work with the children taking up too much of her time?

But Vera spoke up before he could say anything. "I hate that Davy, Kevin, and Kitty won't be able to participate in the church programs anymore. I just need them here at home right now."

Carson gave her a reassuring smile. "I completely understand. And I'm sure they do too."

"I have an idea." Lily leaned forward. "We've just recently added a children's art show to the program. If your children would like to participate, they could still be a part of the celebration and they could work on their pieces here at home."

Of course. Why hadn't he thought of that? "If any of the children are interested, I'll be happy to make sure the materials are delivered here for them, along with the guidelines."

Vera leaned back, wheezing slightly. "You can talk to them about it. If they want to do it, I'm okay with it. Goodness knows they don't get a lot of opportunities these days to just have fun."

Lily stood. "Why don't I do that while you and the pastor finish chatting?"

Carson watched her disappear into the kitchen and found he missed her company. But he resolutely turned back to Vera and tried to gently discuss her needs and offered to pray with her.

ONCE THEY LEFT and were headed back to town, Violet closed her eyes and lifted her face to soak in the sunshine. A fizzy little ball of satisfaction settled in her chest. It had taken a bit of conversational acrobatics, but she'd managed to navigate all of these visits without anyone so much as questioning whether she was really Lily.

When she opened her eyes a moment later, she realized Carson was watching her, a smile twitching his lips.

Feeling her cheeks heat, she quickly grabbed for the first words to take the focus off of herself. "Three of the Franklin children have said they want to participate in the art show."

"Good. I can send the supplies and instructions with Emma."

"How's Mark feeling about the art show? Has he decided to participate?"

The pastor faced forward again. "He hasn't said one way or the other yet." He cut her a sideways look. "But I'm getting a little bit more than single-word answers now."

She smiled. "That sounds like progress."

"Better yet, he's agreed that if anyone shows up tomorrow wanting to participate, he'll help them get started." He raised a brow as his smile broadened. "He even made a suggestion last night—the first time he's volunteered his opinion without being asked."

His obvious fondness for the boy drew an answering smile from her. "And what was his suggestion?"

"That we have a roll of brown paper available so if anyone wants to do a practice sketch first they can do so."

Violet sat up straighter. "Oh, that's a great idea."

He nodded. "I agree. I plan to pick some up when we get back to town."

She almost volunteered to go with him, then realized there was no legitimate reason for her to do so other than she wanted to spend more time with him.

And that really wasn't okay.

Even if she couldn't remember exactly why at the moment.

CARSON STOOD at the door of the church, shaking hands with members of the congregation as they made their exit. All during his sermon he'd been conscious of Lily sitting in her pew beside her aunt. The pair always sat in the fifth pew near the aisle. But today they were joined by a third party. Lily had invited Mark to sit with them, and to his surprise the boy had agreed.

Now, as he accepted murmurs of "good sermon" along with "good day" and a random comment on the weather or the individual's health, he mentally waited for Lily to pass through.

When the trio finally reached him, he shook Adeline's hand first.

"It was a fine sermon, Pastor," Lily's aunt said. "Severe but one we all need to hear."

"Thank you, Mrs. Clemmons. It's a subject I feel very strongly about." The evils of deception was indeed a message he felt passionately about. Possibly because he'd been severely burned by it himself.

Then she was past and it was Lily standing in front of him. The admiration in her expression was quite satisfying. But there was a shadow of some sort there as well. What was troubling her?

Adeline had invited him and Mark to have lunch with them today, so perhaps he would learn more during the visit.

On the carriage ride Friday, during some of the quieter moments, the two of them had made idle conversation that somehow hadn't seemed quite so idle. It wasn't until later that he realized he'd done most of the talking, telling her stories about his childhood growing up on a farm in Ohio, about his years in seminary, and some of his plans for the future. He'd never related those stories before, not even to Ellen, his former wife. But there was something about Lily—a sense of empathy, of having her full attention—that made her so easy to talk to.

That was undoubtably why he now felt a connection to her, new and fragile though it was.

Did she feel it too?

VIOLET RESISTED the urge to kick a pebble as she and Aunt Adeline crossed the street. "The pastor's sermon made me feel more guilty about this masquerade than ever."

Aunt Adeline nodded. "The pastor has very strong feelings about the evils of deception. And not just as a subject for his sermon or in the abstract. He lives it as well."

"What do you mean?"

"Oh, that's right. I keep forgetting you don't know everything your sister does." She glanced Violet's way. "Apparently, when the pastor was much younger, before he even went to seminary, he had a problem with gambling."

Gambling? She had trouble linking that particular vice to Pastor Carson. "But what does that have to do with deception?"

"He wanted his life to be an open book to us, that no one had cause to feel they'd been lied to. So he confessed his history to the deacons before he agreed to serve here. Then he confessed it to the whole congregation along with his vow not to fall into such habits again. He stated he wouldn't accept the post here if the congregation wasn't in total agreement that he was the man for the job."

What courage that must have taken. "And no one objected?"

"There were a few members who were outraged and a few more had reservations, but in the end, because he seemed genuinely repentant, the whole congregation agreed to give him a chance. And he's managed to win everyone over in the time he's been here."

That she could believe—he'd certainly won her over.

"WOULD EITHER of you gentlemen care for another slice of cherry pie?"

Violet watched as the pastor leaned back with a smile of satisfaction. "Thank you, but I'm full. And my thanks for an exceedingly delicious meal."

"Why thank you, Pastor." Aunt Adeline slid her chair back. "Mark, why don't you help me clear the table and do the dishes? My currently one-armed niece here is not much help in that area right now."

Mark stood immediately. "Yes, ma'am."

The older woman turned back to the pastor. "And can I impose on you to do something for me too?"

Carson stood as well. "Of course. What do you need?"

"One of the shelves in my fitting room is wobbly, and I'm worried it'll eventually fall. If you could look at it and see what will be required to repair it, I'd certainly appreciate it."

He nodded. "I'll take a look right now."

She lifted a few dirty dishes from the table. "Lily, would you show him the shelf in question while Mark and I take care of cleaning up?"

Violet resisted the urge to roll her eyes at her aunt's less than subtle maneuver. But she nodded and led the way downstairs and into the fitting room.

"Here it is." Violet waved a hand toward the offending shelf.

The pastor studied it a moment, jiggling it and testing it. Finally he looked up. "I think one well-placed nail would fix this right up."

"Aunt Adeline keeps some tools in the storeroom."

"Lead the way."

Within a few minutes, they had returned to the fitting room with a hammer and nail in hand.

"When you told the congregation about your gambling, was that difficult?" She grimaced. That had come out more abruptly than she intended.

He paused a moment and met her gaze. But instead of a censuring look, he studied her as if looking for something. Then he turned back to his work. "Confessing that you've done something wrong is never easy." His words were almost offhand, as if they were discussing the weather. "But I've learned it's best to be open." He cut her a solemn look. "If for no other reason than that the truth has a way of coming out eventually and it's always better when it comes from the offender than from someone else."

Was he right? Would the truth about her switching places with Lily come to light? If so, the coward in her hoped it wouldn't happen until she was gone.

"If something is weighing on you, you don't have to make a public confession like I did," he added. "You can speak to the person or persons affected. Or you can always speak to a minister or trusted friend for guidance."

Was he volunteering? Of course, in her case he was both the person affected and the minister.

Feeling self-conscious and guilty, Violet put some distance between them but then tripped when she caught her foot on the corner of a box of notions. With her arm in a sling, she was unable to catch herself and ended up on her knees.

Carson was down on his knees at her side in a flash. "Are you all right?" Vertical creases appeared above his nose as he studied her face. "Do you hurt anywhere? Did you reinjure your arm?"

She smoothed her skirt, a totally ridiculous gesture under the circumstances. "I'm fine. The only injury is to my pride."

His concern didn't appear to ease. "Here, let me help you up."

He placed a hand under her left elbow and another at her back, steadying her as she stood. Even though she knew he was just being helpful, the way he held her seemed something more, something almost... intimate. She pushed that thought away—it was just her imagination at work.

But it rattled her enough that her movements were stiff and awkward as he guided her to her feet. It didn't help that she didn't have use of her right arm to help balance her. Which she figured was the reason she ended up stumbling and falling heavily against him. His arms immediately caught her in a hug. For a moment they were locked in an embrace. Her gaze flew to his almost of its own volition, and she saw some strong emotion flicker in his eyes. Her breathing hitched as her heart raced. What was happening to her?

He leaned forward, and for just a heartbeat she thought he was going to kiss her. And that she was most definitely going to let him.

Then he stepped back. "Are you all right?"

She fought to gather her thoughts. "Yes." She shifted her gaze. "Just extremely clumsy today."

He gave a small grin and indicated her sling. "You have a good excuse."

Neither spoke as he finished making repairs. When he was done, he handed the hammer back to her. "I think it's time I thanked your aunt again for her hospitality and the meal and then gather Mark up and take our leave."

"Of course." It seemed he couldn't get away from her fast enough. Well, that was all right by her. She needed some time alone to think.

As soon as he and Mark were gone, Violet told Aunt Adeline she was going to lie down, and she went straight to her room. She flopped down on the bed, staring unseeing at the ceiling. She couldn't possibly have formed feelings for the pastor, she'd only been in town a week. A heartbeat later she realized she was nibbling on her fingernails and jerked her hand away.

How could this have happened? She cut her gaze to the mahogany box that sat on the vanity table, the unconventional pistol sitting inside. "This is all your fault. I know you promised I'd find a man who is steadfast and true, and Carson is most definitely that. But you never warned he might be unavailable to me."

Feeling ridiculous for talking to an inanimate object, she rolled over, turning her back on the pistol. More and more she was regretting that she'd ever convinced Lily to go through with this plan. But they were in too deep now.

There were just three weeks to go. Surely she could get through this.

CARSON TOOK a walk around the backyard, trying to work off some of his restless energy. He couldn't get that moment in the storeroom out of his head. In that heartbeat before she shied away from him like a frightened fawn, she'd looked at him with such breathless yearning it had taken all his control not to tighten his embrace and kiss her.

Was Lily the answer he'd been seeking? She had obviously formed a connection with Mark, one that went both ways. And lately he'd been drawn to her as well.

Now he had some hope that she felt the same way.

He wouldn't push anything until after the celebration—no point in inserting any awkwardness into their activities with the children's programs. And he would do more praying for discernment.

10

Violet was still feeling restless, edgy. Usually she worked off this kind of nervous energy with a round of target practice. She wished now that she'd brought her favorite pistol with her, or any of her guns for that matter. Back when it became obvious she could outshoot most men on her grandfather's ranch, he'd challenged her to try to shoot with her left hand as well as her right. And while she'd never become proficient shooting left-handed, she could do well enough to get by.

Then she remembered that she did have one gun with her. Did that fancy pink-handled revolver shoot straight? Perhaps it was time she put it to the test.

Slipping the pistol and bullets into her skirt pocket, she exited her room. "Aunt Adeline, if you don't mind, I think I'll go for a walk." No point telling her aunt about taking the firearm with her.

Her aunt gave her a concerned look, but only said "Of course, dear."

It was all Violet could do not to run as she stepped out on the sidewalk. She'd spent the past week trying to be Lily—

attempting to mimic her ladylike manner, her feminine movements. Right now she wanted to reclaim her own identity, or one of them anyway. When she slipped into the black mask and costume of the Masked Marvel, she felt daring, confident, commanding even. She really needed that feeling right now.

Barring that, a vigorous walk outdoors and a session of the focused discipline that marksmanship required was the next best thing.

She forced herself to wait until she was near the edge of town before she lengthened and quickened her stride.

She'd spotted an isolated field the other day when she and Pastor Carson had taken the carriage ride to visit the shut-ins. That would suit her purposes nicely. And it shouldn't be more than a twenty-minute walk. Which was fine by her. She hadn't gotten much exercise since she'd arrived here.

As she marched forward, she pulled the pins from her hair and shook it free. Only after she'd taken nearly every pin out did she remember that she wouldn't be able to put it back up with one hand, not neatly anyway. But she'd worry about that later.

By the time she arrived at the field, she felt better, freer. She just wished she'd thought to change out of Lily's fancy church shoes to her own more sensible boots.

Violet glanced around, looking for something she could use for a target. It couldn't be anything too difficult since she wasn't nearly as proficient or even practiced with her left hand as she was with her right.

She spotted a fallen oak tree that would serve the purpose. But she needed to get closer. She marched across the field and managed to snag her hem on some low-growing bramble vines. Having little patience for the encumbrance, she yanked her dress free, ripping it in the process. She should have changed out of this fancy, flowy blue dress before she set out.

She hoped it wasn't one of Lily's favorites, but she'd worry about that later.

She resumed her trek, keeping an eye out for additional brambles, until she was twelve yards from her target. That was closer than her usual targets, but it would do nicely, especially since she was working with an unfamiliar gun and shooting with her left hand.

She gingerly held the gun in her right hand while she loaded it with her left, then swapped hands. She just held it a moment, letting her grip adjust to its feel and weight. It was surprisingly comfortable in her hand.

She set her sights on the center of the horizontal trunk. At least she'd be aiming low to the ground. That way, if she missed the tree, the bullet wouldn't travel far.

Her first shot grazed the side of the trunk. She took a deep breath, aimed carefully once more, determinedly pushing away all thoughts except for the pistol and the target. This time when she fired she had the satisfaction of seeing the bullet drill into the tree.

She backed up several steps and fired again with the same result. She repeated that action of backing up and firing until she'd emptied every bullet from the pistol. As she did so, she thought again of the promise of the pistol. If she believed in such things, which she didn't, she would have to say in her case it had backfired.

She finally lowered the now-empty pistol and nodded in satisfaction. Not bad. With a bit of disciplined practice, she might even be able to add a left-handed shooting element to her act.

Then her sense of satisfaction ebbed. Somehow, she wasn't quite as interested in returning to the traveling show as she once was.

"Impressive."

Violet spun around. Carson! Her fragile calm shattered.

What was he doing here? She fought to get her emotions under control and decided her best course was to go on the offensive. "Are you spying on me?"

WHO WAS THIS PISTOL-TOTING, loose-haired, fierce-eyed woman standing in front of him? Even the lower section of her skirt was torn and raggedy.

She appeared nothing like the fashionable, genteel lady he'd been exchanging pleasantries with for the past fifteen months. It was almost as if they were two different people.

But she was still glaring at him, waiting for an answer.

"Actually, you passed right by my place on your way out of town. You seemed... agitated, and I was concerned you might need some help." Or that the incident in the workroom was at the root of her unrest.

"That was kindly of you, but as you can see I'm fine."

"Are you?"

She held his gaze a moment, and then the defiant glare dimmed and a sort of sheepish grimace replaced it. "I just felt the need for some wide-open space and some challenging activity."

"And this is what you came up with—firing bullets into one of Fred Hamm's trees." And it had looked much less challenging for her than he would have imagined.

She lifted her chin. "It did the trick."

Trying to give himself time to gather his thoughts, he glanced at the pistol in her hand. Nodding toward it, he held out a hand. "Mind if I take a look at that?"

She hesitated a moment. "Do you know how to handle a gun, Pastor?"

He almost grinned at the role reversal. Almost. "I've held a few in my time."

She shrugged and handed it over. "Don't worry, it's empty."

He studied the weapon, intrigued by the unique handle. "It's an unusual-looking firearm. Is it a family heirloom?"

"No, it was a gift."

Who would present her with such a gift? Even though the pink mother-of-pearl on the grip gave it a feminine look, it still wasn't the sort of thing he would have believed Lily would appreciate. But it seemed there were things about Lily he had yet to discover.

"It seems an unusual gift for a well-bred young lady."

She recoiled as if he'd insulted her. Then she straightened. "Actually it was given to me more for the legend attached to it than for its use as a weapon." Her voice had taken on a dry tone.

"Legend?"

She brushed at her skirt, her gaze dropping to her hand. "It's supposed to have matchmaking properties."

Fortunately, he was spared the need to make an immediate response when she waved a hand airily.

"Of course, I don't believe in such things. But apparently someone thought I needed a push in that area."

That he could respond to. "Surely you've never lacked for admirers."

Her cheeks reddened at that, then she shrugged. "Apparently, whoever left this gift for me didn't see it that way."

"So, you don't know who sent it to you?"

She shook her head. "It was dropped off anonymously." Then she straightened. "Let's not talk about it anymore, please."

Was she bothered by the fact that someone was insinuating she needed a matchmaker's help? Or was there something else? Whatever the case, he was happy to change the subject.

"Where did you learn to shoot? And left-handed at that." He handed the pistol back to her as he spoke.

Lily's gaze focused on the weapon as she slipped it back into her pocket. Almost as if she didn't want to meet his gaze. "My grandfather taught me."

"Your grandfather?" Carson frowned in confusion. "I never knew him of course. But I understood he had an accident as a young man that left him with a vision problem."

For a heartbeat Lily froze, then her shoulders sagged as if under a heavy weight. "There's something I need to tell you."

"All right." Carson held very still. There was a doe-like look on her face, as if she'd flee at the least provocation.

She glanced down and brushed at her skirt. Then she glanced his way but didn't quite meet his gaze. "I'm not—" Her head jerked up and swiveled toward the road.

Then he heard it too—the sound of a carriage approaching.

Her hand went to her hair in dismay.

Before either of them could say anything, the carriage came into view and Carson smothered a groan. It was Jenny Filmore and her mother Rowena, the biggest gossip in town.

Without quite realizing that he'd done it, Carson found himself standing protectively in front of Lily. Perhaps the carriage would keep going. Perhaps they wouldn't even notice the two of them standing there.

Unfortunately, almost as soon as he formed the thought, the carriage slowed and then stopped.

"Pastor Davis, is that you?" Rowena Filmore glanced past him with arched brows. "And I do believe I see Lily Mayfield. Whatever takes the two of you out this way?"

Resisting the urge to glance back at Lily, Carson casually crossed his arms. "We decided to take advantage of this lovely spring weather and go for a walk." He straightened and turned back to the would-be sharpshooter. "But I think it's time we head back to town." Perhaps he could learn how she would have finished her sentence on the walk back.

Rowena offered an overly sweet smile. "In that case, why don't you allow us to give you a lift?"

Lily finally found her tongue. "Oh no, that won't be necessary. I don't mind walking."

"But I insist."

Irritated by the woman's insistence but aware that continuing to refuse might raise eyebrows, Carson accepted with what good grace he could muster and escorted a rather stiff Lily to the carriage.

But before he could hand her up, Rowena spoke again. "Lily, I'd like to speak to you about a dress I want to order from your aunt. Why don't you sit up front with me? Jenny, you don't mind giving up your seat do you? You can sit in the back with Pastor Davis."

"Of course." Jenny's smile was bright, eager.

Carson smothered another groan but forced a smile as he stepped forward to help Jenny down. He had an unexpectedly strong urge to protect Lily. Normally he'd say she could hold her own against Rowena's sometimes sharp tongue, but she was in such a strange mood this afternoon, a mood he felt at least partially responsible for.

VIOLET WATCHED Carson help Jenny down from the carriage, wishing she were anywhere else. Her mind was in too much turmoil for her to be able to deal with anything else right now. Had she really almost just blurted out the whole identity-swap story to Carson?

"Lily dear, whatever happened to your hair?"

Violet closed her fist around the river rock in her pocket as she resisted the urge to lift her hand to her hair. Biting her tongue to keep from giving a none-of-your-business reply, she pasted a smile on her face. She wasn't sure what Lily's relationship was with this woman, and she didn't want to burn any bridges. Besides, it wasn't the woman's fault she'd been caught in such a state. "I'm afraid I was walking a bit too vigorously and the pins came out." No point mentioning she helped them along.

"I see. And you can't set it right again with only one hand. You poor dear. Well, we'll get you straight home and hopefully there won't be too many people out and about to notice."

Why did she get the impression the woman was enjoying this?

Carson helped her into the buggy, and a few minutes later the vehicle was in motion.

Before Jenny's mother could ask any more pointed questions, Violet asked one of her own. "So what did you want to discuss about this dress order?"

"Oh that." The woman flicked the reins. "I'm thinking of having a new dress made for the anniversary celebration. I was wondering if your aunt would have time to make it for me or if I'd need to go with ready-made."

"I would need to speak to Aunt Adeline. I'm not sure of her schedule and I definitely haven't been of much use to her since I hurt my arm. Why don't you come by the Emporium first thing in the morning, and she can give you an answer herself?" She tried not to be distracted by the hushed discussion coming from the back seat and Jenny's tittering laughter.

11

Thankfully the ride into town was short, and in a matter of minutes the buggy was drawing up to the dress shop. The vehicle had barely pulled to a stop before Carson hopped out to help her down.

Once she had her feet on the ground, she thanked the pastor and quickly released his hand and turned to Jenny's mother. "Thank you so very much for giving me a ride home. Don't forget to come in to see Aunt Adeline tomorrow so you can get on her schedule." And with a wave she hurried around to the outer staircase. But not before she noted the strange looks she was getting from several folks who were out and about this afternoon.

She'd thought taking a walk and getting in a little target practice would help calm her scattered emotions, but she was more frazzled now than before she set out.

Aunt Adeline was nowhere to be seen when she entered their apartment. Which meant she was either napping or down in the dress shop. Which was fine by Violet.

She went to her room—Lily's room—but couldn't settle down. She paced back and forth across the small room, trying to organize her thoughts. Would it actually have been so terrible if she'd succeeded in telling Carson the truth?

It would have been the honorable thing to do, to come clean and let Carson know who she really was. After all, the whole reason for this charade was to protect the mystery of her Masked Marvel identity. And telling Carson would hardly compromise that.

Then her shoulders sagged and she plopped down on the bed. The problem with that was if Carson looked disapprovingly on their identity swap, it would reflect badly on Lily as well. And Lily had to come back and live in this town among these people. Violet couldn't in good conscience reveal the charade without letting Lily know about it and have a chance to share her feelings.

She moved to the vanity and pulled out a paper and pen. Even though she hadn't heard back from her first letter yet, she'd write another letter to Lily. It was past time to put an end to this whole ill-advised plan.

MONDAY MORNING VIOLET had her letter to Lily ready to go out in that day's mail. In it she'd told Lily they had to meet and change places. She'd made several attempts to explain why and had tossed each one. She'd finally decided to just say that she would explain the reason why when she saw her. She had ended the letter by instructing Lily to send her a telegram with a designation of where and when they should meet to swap their lives back.

Lily would no doubt be relieved to return to Larkin. If things worked out, she could be back in time to enjoy the anniversary celebration.

Coincidentally when the mail carrier arrived, he had a letter for her from Lily, a response to the first letter she'd written no doubt. Was that only five days ago? It seemed so much more time had elapsed.

Unable to wait until the shop closed, Violet retreated behind the counter and opened the letter.

Glad to hear things are going well with you there in Larkin. I've been quite busy here trying to learn everything—it's such a fascinating and excitingly foreign world that you live in. I will write back soon with more detail, but just rest assured that I am having a grand adventure.

I'm so glad you agree that Pastor Carson is a good man. And it's wonderful that you've made a connection with Mark, however small. I know the pastor appreciates it. You will have to fill me in on everything when I return so that I can build on that relationship.

Sorry this is brief, but I need to go. Wyatt sends his best.

Your loving sister,

Lily

PS: Has the pistol worked its matchmaking powers yet?

Violet refolded the letter, feeling oddly dissatisfied. Lily hadn't given her any specifics about her feelings for Carson but had made it obvious she expected to pick up right where she left off when she returned home. And did she really think she could just step in and take her place with Mark? Kids were likely to see through such deceptions faster than adults.

Then Violet took herself in hand. What was wrong with her? Of course when Lily returned, if they were successful with this ruse, no one outside their circle would even know that the switch had taken place. And to make that happen as seamlessly as possible she would have to fill Lily in on everything that had happened while she was here.

Would Carson notice something had changed? Or would he pick up with Lily where the two of them had left off? Not that she was sure where things stood with them at the moment. She was so green at this romance thing. She could have read the signs entirely wrong. Which was what had kept her awake most of the night. All she knew was how she felt, that she had developed feelings for Carson—strong, warm feelings. But Carson was the man Lily—the sister who had put her entire life on hold as a favor to her—had set her sights on.

She had another day to figure out what to do. But whatever she did, there was no way for her to get a happy ending out of this.

Since it was Monday, there was no practice scheduled for the children's program and she had no reason to visit with the pastor or Mark.

Yet she still looked up every time the shop door opened, half expecting to see the pastor walk in, ready to ask her to accompany him on one errand or another. Unfortunately by the time the shop closed, he still hadn't arrived.

"SALLY, that's a nice drawing of the piano." Carson was overseeing the children working on drawings for the art show while Lily led the practice session with the choir. In addition to Sally, there were five other children drawing various aspects of the church interior. Three other children were outside, focusing their creative efforts on drawing the building's exterior.

There were also four children who were working at home on their pieces. That made thirteen children participating altogether, which Carson considered a decent showing for a new program. But what made this even more of a success, at least from his personal perspective, was that Mark had decided to submit a piece of his own. He wouldn't have believed such a change in the boy was possible just a week ago.

And it was mostly thanks to Lily. He glanced her way,

noting how she smiled at her charges, how she got down to Larry's level to speak to him when offering advice.

How had he never noticed this sweeter, gentler side of her before—surely it had always been there?

He'd spent Sunday evening wondering what she'd started to tell him before the Filmores showed up. It had seemed extremely important somehow. He'd decided to confront her on Monday to get answers, but unexpected church obligations had kept him tied up most of the day. She was here today though, so as soon as the children cleared out, he intended to finish the conversation they'd started on Sunday afternoon.

It was important they get everything out in the open between them. Because he'd decided he was ready to go all in and give marriage another chance. Lily was a very different woman than his former wife—she was warm and vital and generous. True, she was more unconventional than he'd realized. If nothing else, that target practice he'd witnessed Sunday was a testament to that. But a bit of eccentricity was not necessarily a bad thing.

The fact that she had barely met his gaze since she arrived at the church didn't worry him overmuch. She was no doubt embarrassed by his catching her at target practice. Or maybe it was her disheveled state that had her feeling mortified. And she'd no doubt built it up in her mind in the day and a half that had elapsed since. She just needed a little reassurance that he didn't think any less of her for it. And he was certainly ready to give her that.

So as soon as practice was over, he approached her. "Miss Mayfield, can I have a word with you?"

"Of course." There was a distinct lack of enthusiasm in her tone. "Practice today went very well, don't you think? I believe the children are nearly ready."

He nodded. "I agree."

Before he could broach the subject he was most interested

in, she spoke up again. "And it's exciting to see so many children participating in the art program." She wet her lips. "Now if you'll excuse me, I need to head back to the Emporium."

She appeared to be babbling. He needed to pull her back. "Surely you can spare a few more minutes."

"I don't—"

He held a hand up. "If you're uncomfortable because of what happened on Sunday—"

"No, I mean yes. I mean, I should have been more conscious of my surroundings."

"What I was trying to say is you don't need to feel uncomfortable for showing me that side of yourself, even if it was unintentional. We all need to find a way to just free ourselves from the conventions occasionally."

"Even you, Pastor?"

He grinned. "Especially me."

"And what do you do when you're letting off a bit of steam?"

He shrugged. "I chop firewood."

"That's hardly unconventional."

"But it does let me work off any excess feelings when I need to." He shifted to a more serious tone. "Back there in the field on Sunday, you started to tell me something. What was it?"

She went very still, and there was a trapped-animal look in her eyes. "I can't..." She lifted a hand and then let it fall limply at her side.

Back in the storeroom on Sunday she'd asked him how hard it had been for him to confess about his gambling. Was there something she was struggling with confessing? Perhaps if he shared something personal, something painful, it would give her the courage to do the same.

"The other day we talked about the fact that I'm a widower."

She nodded.

"Ellen passed away about two years ago, four months before I moved here."

She nodded again.

Carson tried to relax, to not give in to the tension that threatened to choke him every time he thought of his wife's deep betrayal.

Lord, please let me do this in a way that allows her to see her own way forward.

Feeling calmer, he indicated she should take a seat on the front pew. "The details of her death are common knowledge, at least in the town where we lived at the time. What *isn't* common knowledge is that Ellen and I did not have a very happy marriage."

VIOLET SAT BACK, her desire to put distance between them suddenly forgotten. Why was he telling her this?

"I was still in seminary when I met Ellen. She was the daughter of my mentor. Ellen wasn't classically beautiful, but there was a demure sort of loveliness about her. She was a very proper, very charitable, very learned young lady. She was also a children's Sunday school teacher, and she spent her spare time making blankets for the needy. She knew the text of the Bible as well as I did, if not more so. In other words, Ellen was the perfect pastor's wife."

"Is that why you married her?" Didn't love come into it at all?

"In part. After all, a pastor must be above reproach. And by extension, so should his wife." He rubbed the back of his neck. "But I did love her in my own way. I couldn't have married her otherwise."

Not a deeply romantic story but she supposed that was just fairy-tale thinking.

"But she wasn't completely honest with me," he continued.

She saw his jaw work and realized this was a difficult story for him to tell. "You don't need to say anything more. It's none of my business—"

"Actually, I'd like for you to know. A few days ago you asked me how it was to tell the congregation about my gambling. Do you remember what I told you?"

"You said that the truth has a way of coming out eventually."

"Yes, and it's always best if you deliver your truths rather than have someone else reveal it." His smile had a resigned air about it. "Not only does it keep you from having egg on your face but it also eases that little tangled ball of nerves that lodges itself in your gut whenever you start trying to deceive people."

Violet nodded, but inside she was squirming. Did he suspect she was keeping something from him?

He paced a few steps, then returned. "As it turns out, Ellen would have preferred to take a vow of celibacy, but her parents had drilled it into her head that it was her Christian duty to marry and to mother children. Something I didn't find out until *after* we were married." He tugged his cuff, glancing down as he did so. "I hope you don't find this too indelicate, but she viewed the marriage act as something distasteful to be endured, not as an expression of love between a husband and wife."

Violet felt her face heat. But despite her embarrassment at the nature of his revelation, her overwhelming emotion was sympathy for the situation he'd found himself in. It was all she could do not to reach out and touch him. "Oh Carson, I'm so sorry." It was a heartbeat later that she realized she'd used his given name. But if he noticed, he didn't say anything.

"Thank you. But I didn't tell you all that to elicit your sympathy. I wanted you to understand why I feel so strongly about the importance of honesty."

Violet felt as if she were smothering. She had to get out of here.

She stood abruptly. "I truly appreciate you trusting me with your story, and I want you to know you can trust me not to gossip or mention it in any way. But I really do need to get back now." And before he could try to stop her, she'd turned and hurried from the church.

DISAPPOINTED, Carson watched her leave. Whatever she'd been about to share with him Sunday afternoon she'd apparently thought better of it.

Was it a matter of trust?

Or was there something else at play?

V iolet did her best to avoid Carson for the rest of the day on Tuesday and on Wednesday. She saw him at the committee meeting, of course, and reported on the handbill she and Mark had designed. But she'd made a point to arrive at the last minute and scurry out as soon as it was over, so there was no opportunity for casual conversation with Carson.

If that made her a coward, then so be it.

When she found the telegram from Lily waiting for her back at the Emporium Wednesday afternoon, she almost sagged in relief. Lily had agreed to meet with her, setting the place as Shreveport and the time as Friday afternoon.

This would all be over soon, and she could go back to her old life. It was what she'd been hoping for the past few days. And it really was for the best.

So why did she feel so empty?

"Miss Mayfield."

Violet, who'd been watching Carson working with his group of children, turned at Mark's hail. "Yes? Do you need some help?"

"No, ma'am. I finished my piece for the art show. But I wanted to give you something."

Violet's chest warmed at those words and the earnest expression on the boy's face. "I like surprises."

He pulled a sheet of paper from his notebook, scuffing his feet nervously as he did so. "The other day you told me you knew how it's okay to hold on to things just for yourself until you're ready to share."

She nodded, watching him intently.

"It's the kind of thing my mother used to tell me. It's like you really could see what I was feeling, just like she always could."

"Oh, Mark, that's the most wonderful thing you could say to me."

"Anyway, I'm ready to share now, with you at least." And he held out the paper to her.

She accepted it and found herself staring at a large tree with spreading branches covered in vines. It was only when she looked closer that she saw a rickety-looking, rudimentary treehouse. The picture wasn't polished and perfect, but the level of detail he was able to show without cluttering the picture was remarkable, especially for a nine-year-old.

"Mark, this is amazing. I'm going to frame it and keep it where I can see it."

He quit scuffing the toe of his shoe and stood a little taller.

"Is this an actual place or did it come from your imagination?"

"It's real. I found it one day when I was following a dog I wanted to draw. It's on the back end of a field that has a big fallen log in it."

"Oh, I think I know that place, but I never saw this."

He nodded. "It's hard to spot. That's what makes it special."

"Well, I think this drawing is special. And since you've given it to me, I'd like to give you something special in return so you'll have a piece of me as well." She reached in her pocket and pulled out the water-polished rock. "I know this doesn't look like much and it's not something I created, but I've had this since I was five years old. I found it next to a creek at the end of one of those days when everything seems perfect and you don't have a care in the world. I thought it was the most beautiful thing I'd ever seen. Even my daddy said it was special when he saw it." She pulled herself back out of her reverie. "Anyway, whenever I've had a really rough day, I'd take this stone out and it reminds of that day when everything was right in my world and I'd start to feel better. I'd be honored if you'd accept it and maybe think of today and of me when you look at it." She handed it over without a qualm. It was as if she'd been holding on to it all this time for just this moment.

He took it from her and turned it over in his hands, examining it from every angle. "I think you're right—this is a very special rock."

Unable to resist, she gave him a quick hug, and to her surprise he hugged her back for just a heartbeat. Then he squirmed out of her grasp and returned to the group still working on their art projects.

Why oh why couldn't she have been up front with Carson to start with? What was that old saying? *Oh what a tangled web we weave...*

When she glanced up, she realized Carson was watching her. How much had he seen?

Feeling suddenly self-conscious, she turned away and carefully tucked the drawing Mark had given her into her tote, then busied herself admiring the children's artwork until it was time for her to work with the choir.

"ALL RIGHT, everyone, you did very well today." Violet smiled at the children. It was surprising how much she was going to miss them. "I'm so proud of how hard you are all working. We only have three practice sessions left before the big day, but I am absolutely confident that you're going to not only be ready but that your performance will be amazing."

As the children broke ranks and prepared to leave, Violet turned to Carson, who was helping the young artists put away their supplies.

"Those of you who are finished with your piece, leave it on one of the first few pews on the right side of the aisle. If you aren't yet done, leave it on a pew on the left side of the aisle."

Violet watched the way he interacted with the children, content to wait until he was done. The kids responded well to him. Even Mark had thawed considerably.

Finally the last of the children were headed for the door, and she cleared her throat.

He met her gaze and smiled. It struck her that he might think she was ready to tell him her secrets as he'd hoped when they'd spoken Tuesday.

If so, she was about to disappoint him. "I just wanted to let you know, something has come up and Aunt Adeline and I will be out of town tomorrow and most of Saturday. That means I won't be here for the next practice session."

Disappointment flashed across his features, but it changed almost immediately as his brow drew down in concern. "I hope nothing untoward has happened."

"Not at all. Just a bit of family business we need to see to."

"I'm glad it's nothing serious. And don't worry. I'm sure I can manage the children on my own for this one session. If nothing else, Brenda has mentioned on several occasions she'd be happy to help."

Violet felt a flash of something very like jealousy. But she was being ridiculous. After today she wouldn't be around any longer. She quickly turned the conversation. "Mark appears to have taken his responsibility with this art program very seriously. I see him guiding and interacting with the other children during our practice sessions, and I think he's really finding his footing."

Carson's smile turned warm and satisfied. "I've noticed it too. And it's starting to affect other aspects of his life."

"I just want to say, I'm so happy to see that the two of you are beginning to find some common ground."

"Speaking of common ground, was that your polished stone you gave him?"

So he *had* seen. "Yes. It served its purpose with me. I figured I'd pass it on to someone else who might appreciate it."

"That was very thoughtful."

She merely shrugged, said a quick goodbye, and headed for the exit.

As she walked away, she realized that was the last conversation she'd ever have with the pastor. Then she said a silent prayer that she could make it home without bawling.

WHEN SHE'D STAYED BEHIND to speak to him, Carson had hoped she was finally going to confide in him. He couldn't say he wasn't disappointed that she hadn't, but she was beginning to come around, he could feel it.

He still couldn't believe she'd given her stone to Mark. Did the boy know what a treasured keepsake she'd given him? And why had Lily done it? He'd only caught the tail end of their interaction, and he hadn't heard any of the conversation, so he wasn't sure what had prompted the gift-giving.

But it was a good sign, an indication that she felt she had a special relationship with Mark, perhaps even a maternal one?

"ARE you absolutly sure this is what you want to do, dear?"

They were finally pulling into the train depot in Shreveport, and Aunt Adeline had asked about a dozen different variations of that same question during the long train ride. Violet had tried to convince her before they ever boarded back in Larkin that she could travel alone, that it wasn't necessary for the dressmaker to shut down the Emporium just to accompany her on this trip. But Aunt Adeline had insisted.

"Yes, I'm absolutely sure." She lifted her chin. "I guess I didn't give enough thought to the fact that I'd be lying to everyone around me while I was in Larkin. It just feels so wrong. My stomach is all tied in knots, and I can hardly look people in the face." Especially Carson. "No, it's better that I go back to my life and let Lily go back to hers."

"There's always another option—you can return as Violet and tell the truth."

"I think I've already burned that bridge." She stood. "Now it looks like we've arrived. Make sure you have everything before we disembark."

The first person she saw when she stepped off the train was Wyatt. She quickly headed across the platform, meeting him halfway and giving him a one-armed hug. "It's so good to see you. I should have known you'd accompany Lily."

He quickly hugged her back, then took a small step away. "You're looking good, Vi. But what's this about wanting to end the swap early? I've never known you to be a quitter."

"I have my reasons."

"Let her be, Wyatt." Lily extricated herself from her own bear hug with Aunt Adeline. "Violet and I need to talk this out since we're the ones affected."

To Violet's surprise, Wyatt lifted his palms and didn't say more.

Lily turned back to their aunt. "I've reserved some nice rooms at the Hotel Ashworth, which is just a few blocks away. Why don't you let Wyatt escort you there while Violet and I chat? Then we can all get together for dinner."

"Of course, dear. I'm always happy to have a handsome man at my side."

Wyatt stepped forward and offered her his arm. "My pleasure. Shall we?"

Violet watched them walk away, strangely reluctant to face Lily just yet.

Finally her sister spoke up. "That bench over there seems to be relatively private. Why don't we sit there while we talk?"

Violet followed Lily to the aforementioned bench, studying the garment her sister was wearing. It was one of her dresses, yet not. "What's that you're wearing?" she asked.

Lily spread her skirt as she sat. "Don't you recognize it?" she asked smugly. "It's one of your dresses."

"It certainly doesn't look the same as it did last time I saw it."

"I just took the skirt in a bit and added some sleeker trim."

Violet dropped the pretense that she was concerned with fashion. "I take it you didn't tell Wyatt what this is all about."

"No, I figured you and I should discuss it first. Not that I know much myself. You were pretty vague." She scooted over and patted the spot beside her for Violet to sit. "So, talk. Why do we need to swap back now?"

Violet put her face in her hands. "I just can't take this constant need to evade and deceive anymore."

"You knew what was going to be required before you even proposed this plan to me. What's changed?"

"But I didn't realize it was going to be so difficult." Wasn't Lily facing the same problem?

Lily met and captured her gaze, staring into her eyes with the intensity of someone trying to read answers there. It was all Violet could do not to look away.

"No," her sister said slowly. "There's something else, something you're not telling me."

Violet picked at her skirt. "Pastor Carson and I have—I mean I think we have... gotten sort of... um, *close* this past week." She rushed to reassure her sister. "I know you have your heart set on him, but he still thinks I'm you, so you should be okay."

Lily was frowning, but strangely she looked more puzzled than angry. "What do you mean by close?"

Violet didn't quite meet her sister's gaze. "Close in that we've been spending a lot of time together. We've told each other personal stories about our pasts. We've told each other about our hopes for the future." And I spend nearly every waking moment thinking about him. And I dream about what it would have felt like if he had kissed me in the storeroom last Sunday.

Trying to shake off those thoughts, she waved her free hand. "Of course he thought he was sharing all of this with you."

The silence lasted several heartbeats, and Violet finally looked up. She found Lily studying her with an unreadable expression on her face.

"It sounds like you've developed some feelings for Pastor Carson."

Violet tried hard not to squirm. "It doesn't matter. Like I said, he thinks I'm you, so it's you he feels he's grown closer to, not me. And if we swap places right now, he need never know the truth."

"I'm not so sure that's true."

"What do you mean?"

Lily took her hand in both her own. "I know I told you I had my eye on Pastor Carson. But we've never done much more than exchange pleasantries, no matter how much I flirted with him. It sounds like in the two weeks you've known him though, you've managed to get closer to him than I have in over a year of our acquaintance."

Was her sister deliberately misunderstanding? "But don't you see? To him this is just an extension of the time he's known you. I've only been able to develop this closeness because of the friendship the two of you had before we swapped. There's no way he could have developed any sort of feelings for me in less than two weeks, assuming he actually has. And if Carson knew the real me, it definitely wouldn't have happened."

Lily dropped her hand and tilted her head slightly to one side. "Carson is it?"

Violet felt her cheeks heat, but Lily didn't give her a chance to respond.

"Do you really think so little of him that you believe he would judge you by your upbringing or how you get by?"

Violet lifted her chin. "All I know is he thinks I'm an elegant, fashionable, well-bred young lady who has roots that go deep in Larkin. He also has a deep dislike for folks who take an end-justi-fies-the-means approach to difficult situations. Which is exactly what I did when I set this plan to swap places in motion." Her shoulders sagged. "Why didn't I just disappear for four weeks? Sure, Wyatt and I would've lost wages and perhaps our jobs alto-gether, but I would have had a clear conscience at the end."

"You *did* learn quite a bit about the pastor, didn't you?"

Then her gaze dropped to Violet's hands. "I see your nails are looking a bit ragged."

Not sure how to respond, Violet held her peace.

After a moment, Lily straightened. "My answer is no."

Violet felt her brows draw down. "What do you mean? Your answer to what?"

"No, I will not swap places with you today."

That was something she hadn't anticipated. "But—"

"You need to go back and talk to the pastor. Tell him the truth of who you are, what we did, and why we did it. You owe it to him, and to yourself, to give him the opportunity to decide for himself how he wants to deal with this."

Violet couldn't believe what she was hearing. "But what about the feelings you have for him? You can build on what we started." The words were like self-inflicted wounds. "It's you he really wants, not me."

"I disagree. He displayed very little interest until you showed up, and then it sounds like the attraction was almost instantaneous. And mutual."

Lily was reading way too much into the situation. "That's partly because he was impressed by how I got through to Mark."

"Perhaps that's so. But again that's something you were able to do that I couldn't." She shrugged. "And if the only reason he values you is for what you've done for Mark, then at least you'll know that as well. But you'll never know how he truly feels about *you* if you don't introduce him to the real you."

"But if he can't get past my deception, it'll spill over on you too. Surely you don't want to risk coming home to that."

She waved a hand dismissively. "Don't worry about me. It may be a bit awkward at first, but I'm a big girl and my friends in Larkin know me well. I'll just explain that I was having a grand adventure—which I am by the way."

"But I don't know if I can do this." Violet couldn't stop the near wail underlying her words.

"The way you feel about him, is he worth fighting for?"

Violet sat up straighter. "Yes, he is."

"Then there's your answer." She shrugged. "Besides, if it makes you feel better, now that I've put some distance between the pastor and me, I find I'm not as romantically attracted to him as I thought I was."

"Does this mean you've found someone else?"

Lily grinned and gripped the bench on either side of her skirt. "What it means is I'm having fun. When I agreed to this swap, you promised me four weeks, and I want to enjoy every bit of that time." Then she turned the focus back on Violet's dilemma. "I know it's scary to have to confess something like this, especially when you value the opinion of the person you wronged, but in the end, it's better that he hears it from you face-to-face." Lily stood. "Now come on, let's see when the next train to Larkin departs."

It sounded like there was no getting around this. For good or ill, she was headed back to face the music.

13

Once Violet decided to return and talk to Carson, she hadn't wasted time. There was a train leaving at 9:50 that evening, and she'd determined to be on it. She had encouraged Aunt Adeline to get a good night's sleep at the hotel and make the trip back the next day, but the older woman had pooh-poohed that idea. "I can sleep as easily on the train as in a hotel, and this will let me open up the Fashion Emporium for half a day."

And true to her word, Aunt Adeline had slept most of the trip.

Not so Violet. The train ride back to Larkin had seemed interminable. Dozens of different ways this meeting could go —most of them disastrous—had played and replayed themselves in her mind, making the thirteen-hour train ride seem twice that.

But now that they were pulling into the station, it felt like time was speeding up, pushing her relentlessly forward to the final act. The question was, was this play to be a comedy or a tragedy?

As they began gathering their things, Violet turned to her

aunt. "I need to see the pastor as soon as I can."

Aunt Adeline gave her an understanding smile. "Of course, dear. Don't worry about me. I'm quite capable of getting myself home. And I'll see to your bag as well."

Giving her aunt a grateful smile, Violet set off at a fast clip. She'd look for him first at the church. The practice session would have wrapped up about twenty minutes ago, but he might still be there. If not there she supposed she'd try his home next. If he wasn't there, surely his housekeeper could tell her where to find him.

It wasn't until she approached the church itself that Violet's steps slowed. She'd felt she was prepared to face Carson with the truth, but now that the time was upon her, her stomach was fluttering wildly and her thoughts were just as scattered. What did she say exactly? Hello, I'm not who you think I am. I've been lying to you for the past two weeks.

She took a couple of deep breaths, said a quiet prayer for help in finding the right words, then opened the door and stepped inside.

He was here. So was Mark. That might present a little problem. She would tell Mark the truth as well, of course. But she'd prefer to tell Carson first, and alone.

It was Mark who noticed her first. The boy's face lit up, and he lifted a hand in greeting. "Hello, Miss Mayfield. You're back early."

Violet returned his smile. "That I am. But it seems I wasn't early enough to help with practice."

As she spoke to Mark, Violet had kept Carson in her peripheral vision. She'd been waiting for the moment when he would glance up and see her, hoping she'd see that warm smile that always made her feel special, as if he'd reserved it just for her. But when he did finally meet her gaze, the smile was absent. In its place was a measuring look, one that seemed to find her lacking in some way.

Was he still upset that she hadn't responded to his attempts to draw her out? Hopefully she could take care of that now. She only hoped it wasn't too late.

Before she reached them, Carson turned to Mark. "Would you mind waiting for me in the office? Miss Mayfield and I have some things to discuss."

Mark must have heard the same measured tone in Carson's voice that she did because the boy shot an uncertain look from one to the other of them, then answered with a nod and a "Yes, sir" before he made his exit.

"Hello." It felt inadequate, but his continued silence and scrutiny was unnerving.

He nodded. "Miss Mayfield."

There was none of the familiar lightness to his tone. Had something happened while she was away?

She still wasn't sure how to broach the subject, especially with him in this strange mood, so she opened with something innocuous. "I'm so sorry I had to miss the practice today. How did the children do?"

"They did fine. I asked Brenda Kester to step in for you."

"Oh." For some reason she'd thought he'd lead them himself since it was just for the one session.

"Yes." He returned to loading the art supplies into their boxes. "In fact, she's volunteered to take over for you if you're unable to continue working with the children."

That comment, and the way he said it as if it were an actual option set her back on her heels. "That was very generous of her," she said warily. "But I'm back now, so that shouldn't be necessary."

He met her gaze with a hard one of his own. "And just *who* is it that's back?"

The butterflies in Violet's stomach turned into bats with sharp raking claws.

He knew!

14

Surely there was another explanation—he couldn't know. "What do you mean?"

"I heard something interesting yesterday when I was making the rounds of the shut-ins. I stopped by to visit Henry Stebbins, and he started reminiscing about his glory days. Your grandfather's name came up. And in case you're confused, I'm referring to Wallace Mayfield, the grandfather who was born and raised right here in Larkin."

"Of course." She could barely get the words out past the lump in her throat.

"During our discussion, I remarked that Wallace must have been quite a character what with him having taught his grand-daughter to shoot."

Oh no.

"Imagine my surprise when he told me I must be mistaken, that Wallace had a very deep dislike of firearms of any sort. Henry did mention though that he thought he'd heard that your other grandfather lived on a ranch and led a very rugged life. And then he added that Lily's sister grew up there." His lips compressed. "I just assumed when you told me you had a sister you were separated from when your parents died you meant she'd passed too, but you meant actually separated didn't you?"

Unable to speak, Violet nodded.

"And you aren't just sisters, you're identical twins."

Again she nodded.

"So who are you?"

"My name is Violet Taylor."

"So Violet Taylor, did you and Lily just decide to swap places on a lark?"

"No, of course not. We wouldn't do that."

Before she could explain further, he pushed on. "You felt it was okay to deceive everyone this way. To deceive me. I told you about my wife, about how she tricked me into marrying her, how she lied by omission and made a mockery of our marriage. And still you did this."

"I wanted to tell you. I just... couldn't, not until now."

"Now that I've already figured it out you mean. I gave you every chance."

"Carson, please let me—"

"Is your arm even hurt?"

She stiffened. "Yes, of course it is. I wouldn't make up such a thing."

"You do hear the irony in that don't you?"

Immediately her indignation was replaced with a sense of defeat.

"How much longer had the two of you planned to carry on this charade?"

"Another two weeks or so." She had to try to distance her sister from this. "But Lily didn't—"

He didn't let her finish. "I think it best we just let Brenda take over with the children's choir. After all, it was your sister who signed on for this task, not you." The note of bitterness that had crept into his voice only made his rejection harder to bear.

"I don't mind. In fact, I enjoy—"

"Working with children requires a certain dedication and character, a resolve to follow through on commitments. It's not something to take lightly. I believe Brenda has the requisite qualities to bring that to the position."

"I understand." He was apparently ready to cut all ties.

"Good. Now if you'll excuse me, I need to work on my sermon for tomorrow." And with that he turned and walked away in the direction of the office.

She dropped into the front pew, not sure she could trust herself to walk back to the dress shop just yet without breaking down. How had this day turned from guardedly hopeful to nightmarish in the space of a few minutes?

When she'd asked him about how difficult it had been for him to confess his gambling to the congregation, one of the things he'd told her was that the truth had a way of coming out eventually and it was best for the offender to bring it to light him or herself.

She'd waited too long, and the worst had happened. After what he'd told her about his former wife, she couldn't really blame him for his reaction.

What did she do now? She couldn't go back to the circus—even if she no longer cared about keeping her performance identity secret. Lily had insisted she have her four-week adventure. But she couldn't imagine staying here two more weeks, taking the chance of running into Carson at every turn. Maybe she'd just find another location to just wait things out. It didn't much matter where.

Wearily she got to her feet and moved to the door. She prayed she could reach the privacy of her room before the tears let loose.

CARSON DIDN'T GO to his office immediately. He didn't want to face Mark until he had himself back under control. He leaned against the wall in the hall and closed his eyes.

How could he have considered marrying again, and to another woman who kept her true self hidden from him? He must be the world's most gullible man to be betrayed this way, not once but twice.

The next two weeks couldn't pass quickly enough. True, Lily had participated in this charade as well, but he could ignore her presence a lot easier than he could Violet's.

How had he not seen that this was a different woman than the one he'd known for a year and a half? The sling had thrown him off, of course. Still, the differences in personality, the minor flubs she'd made with names those first few days, the way she'd connected with Mark—those should have at least raised some suspicions.

He scrubbed a hand across his face. He probably could have handled that confrontation a bit better a few minutes ago —he blamed it on the lack of sleep from the night before. And he certainly hadn't expected to see her until later today or tomorrow at church service, so she'd caught him unawares.

For a minute the memory of that lost, holding-back-the-tears expression on her face haunted him. But he shook it off. She'd just reacted to getting caught, nothing more.

He pushed away from the wall, schooled his expression, and went to tell Mark it was time to go home for lunch.

15

As Carson preached from the podium Sunday morning on the sin inherent in lies of omission, he kept his gaze carefully averted from Violet.

But that didn't mean he was unaware of her every move— it was as if some sense in him was attuned to her. She sat on the right-hand side of her aunt as always, but her back was ramrod straight and her gaze was locked forward though not on him but on a point over his right shoulder.

Mark sat on her right. Carson hadn't wanted to tell Mark of Violet's duplicity, not when the boy was finally starting to open up. And he hadn't been able to come up with another reason to keep the boy from sitting with them.

After the service, he stood at the door as usual, shaking hands with the members of the congregation as they made their exits. All he could think about as he exchanged pleasantries with one congregant after the other was how Violet would handle it when it was her turn.

How would he?

He braced himself as her aunt stepped up with Violet and Mark right behind her. Adeline nodded pleasantly. "That was a strong sermon, Pastor, a nice follow-up to last Sunday's sermon."

"Thank you, Mrs. Clemmons." How much did she know? Surely she must know her nieces had swapped places, but how much did she know of what had happened since?

But the woman wasn't through speaking. "And while I think hearing the serious spiritual harm negative actions like deception and lies of omission can do is important for the soul-deep well-being of the congregation, perhaps next Sunday you could focus a little time on the merits of positive, virtuous actions, such as love and forgiveness."

This was delivered with a sunny smile and artless tone, and she moved on immediately without waiting for a response. So why did he feel as if he'd been judged and found wanting?

Then Violet was standing in front of him. If one didn't look too closely, she seemed collected, serene even. But a closer look showed red-rimmed eyes and a certain tension in her jaw. She had a hand on Mark's shoulder, and she smiled though her gaze didn't quite meet his. "In case you don't already know this, in addition to being a fine artist, Mark here is a very good singer." Her gaze lowered to the boy with a more genuine smile.

"Is that so?"

She nodded. "When he decides to sing out, it's definitely a joyous sound."

Mark was squirming under the praise.

Apparently feeling she'd said enough, Violet gave them both a nod and quickly followed her aunt down the stairs.

Carson only had a heartbeat to digest how she'd looked and sounded before he had to turn and shake the hand of Jed Tomlinson as well as all the other congregants lined up behind him. Which was fine with him. Spending any time at all thinking about Violet wasn't good for his state of mind.

Once the last of the congregants left, he and Mark walked

the four blocks to their home. He had turned down the three invitations he'd received for lunch, feeling he wasn't going to be great company today. As they walked down sidewalks, Carson mentally debated whether to tell Mark about Violet's deception. Then Mark took the decision out of his hands.

"Don't you and Miss Mayfield like each other anymore?"

Caught by surprise, Carson didn't answer directly, instead asking a question of his own. "Why do you ask?"

"Bobby Nelson said Miss Mayfield wasn't going to work with the choir or art show anymore, that you had asked Miss Kester to take her place." Mark kicked a rock. "I asked Miss Mayfield about it this morning. She said she needed to spend more time at her aunt's dress shop."

Carson raised a brow. "And you didn't believe her?"

Mark turned the tables on him and didn't answer. "During service this morning, she didn't look at you the way she did before. And ever since she got back yesterday, neither one of you smile at *anybody* anymore. And both of you get all stiff when you're together and seem like you can't wait to get away."

The boy was a lot more perceptive than he'd given him credit for. Carson chose his next words carefully. "While I'm sure it's true that Miss Mayfield wants to spend more time with her aunt, you are also correct in thinking something else has happened. But you'll just have to content yourself with the answer that it's not something I want to talk about right now."

Mark didn't say anything for a moment. Then he looked up and met Carson's gaze, his eyes wide and his hands stuffed into his pants pocket. "Is it okay if *I'm* still friends with her?"

Carson hesitated between one step and the next. How in the world should he answer that? On the one hand, he was no longer certain of Violet's character, and she had admitted that she and Lily would swap places again in a couple of weeks. On the other hand, he really didn't believe Violet would knowingly hurt Mark and Mark was only just now learning to trust again. Before the silence could draw out too long, he nodded. "Of course." He'd just have to make sure that the time Mark spent in Violet's company was severely limited. Hopefully, in time, other relationships would take the place of Violet's.

After lunch, Mark settled in with his sketch pad and Carson headed out for a walk in the garden. He was in the right here of course. He had told her specifically about the deception his first wife had carried out on him and the unhappy results. It hadn't been easy to discuss something so personal, so painful. Dredging up those memories had resurrected feelings he'd hoped to never experience again.

And she didn't think enough of him to confess a deception she and her sister had pulled off as a lark. And yes, he saw repentance in her eyes when he looked at her now, but how could he trust that it was anything more than being sorry she'd gotten caught. Would she even have said anything when she and Lily decided to swap back? Or would she have gone on with her life—whatever that turned out to be—without giving him and Mark another thought?

Still, her aunt's words niggled at him, still whispered that there was more to consider here. The Bible taught that forgiveness was something that should be freely and abundantly given. When he counseled others who had issues with holding grudges, he tried to help them see that forgiveness did as much, if not more, to bring a sense of peace to the person offering it as to the person it was offered to. It was certainly easier to hand out that guidance than to accept it for himself.

Carson sat down on the garden bench and bowed his head. He did what he should have done when he learned the truth on Friday. He prayed.

He wasn't sure how long he sat there, but Carson finally stood and headed for his study. He felt the need to immerse himself in scripture, to find his footing again. He could—and should—forgive Violet. That didn't require him to look on her as a potential wife again. It did require that he scrub the bitterness from his heart.

As soon as Carson opened the door to his study, he could tell someone had been in here. Papers on his desk that had been in a nice tidy pile were now messily stacked. And his Bible, which normally sat on the right-hand corner of the desk, was now near the middle and lay open.

Then he saw the letter, the one he kept tucked safely and secretly away in the Bible, sitting open next to the Bible, and he felt his world tilt off-center.

He had to find Mark.

16

"I refuse to let you hide in our apartment and nurse your hurts for two weeks."

Violet looked up, stung by her aunt's lack of sympathy. "Actually I was thinking about going away."

"Humph! Don't be ridiculous. You are going to stay right here and hold your head up high."

"Why would I want to do that?"

"Because you're not a coward. And because it's Lily's reputation you're upholding."

She hadn't thought about that. Her aunt was right. She was stuck here whether she wanted to be or not.

Seeing Carson this morning had been torture. His drawn expression and impassioned delivery of the sermon had cut at her, had made her want to both comfort him and run away. Thank goodness she'd had Mark to act as a buffer of sorts when they exited the church.

There would be two more Sunday services during her time here, so those would be the only times she'd really have to see Carson. The only times she'd actually have to go out at all, regardless of what Aunt Adeline said. Then she groaned.

There'd also be the anniversary celebration. There was no way she could skip that without causing talk.

A knock at the outer door provided a welcome interruption to Violet's thoughts. She glanced over at her aunt. "Are you expecting a visitor?"

Adeline set her book down in her lap. "No, but company is always welcome. Would you see who it is, dear?"

"Of course." When Violet opened the door, to her surprise it was Carson standing there. A very worried-looking Carson. "Carson! I mean Pastor. What are you—? I mean come in."

But he raked a hand through his hair, his expression grim. "No time for that. I just wanted to see if Mark was here by any chance."

"Mark? No, why?" Then she stiffened as she connected his words to his worried expression. "Has something happened to him?"

"I'm not sure, but he's missing. I haven't seen him since lunch. I think he may have run away."

Why did he think Mark had run away after only being out of his sight for a couple of hours? "Perhaps he's just somewhere with his sketchbook and lost track of time."

"I don't think so. And I've looked everywhere I can think of." He was clearly worried.

"Let me change my shoes and I'll help search."

But he shook his head. "No, but thank you. I just wanted to make sure he wasn't here. Please let me know if something occurs to you."

Didn't he trust her to help? "Of course." She placed a hand on his arm. "Don't worry, he's an intelligent, resourceful boy. He'll be okay."

Carson nodded, looking at her hand on his arm, his expression unreadable as his jaw worked.

Had she overstepped? She removed her hand and moved back slightly. "I'll be praying as well."

He nodded. "Thank you." And then he was gone.

She slowly walked back to the parlor. At least he was talking to her again and there'd been none of that disappointment and anger in his expression that she'd seen earlier. Of course it might have just been temporarily pushed aside by his worry over Mark.

She returned to the sitting room and explained to Aunt Adeline what had just occurred. After another ten minutes of worrying about both Mark and Carson, Violet popped up from her seat. "This is ridiculous. I can't just sit here. I have to help."

Aunt Adeline gave her a mild, slightly befuddled look. "I know it's difficult, dear, but the pastor asked you to stay here in case Mark comes by."

"I know, but if that does happen, you'll be here." And without waiting for a response, Violet hurried to her room to change clothes.

Ten minutes later she was headed down the back stairs dressed in her own clothes, not Lily's. Since her secret was already out, there was no longer any reason to pretend she was anyone other than herself.

And while she'd been changing, she remembered something. Something that might lead her to where Mark could be. The thing was, what did she do with that information? She hated to get Carson's hopes up in case she was wrong. Besides, she wasn't quite sure where to find Carson right now.

No, it was probably best that she check out her hunch first.

Violet headed out at a fast clip, using the most direct path, staying off the main streets. The ground was rocky and uneven, making the going more difficult.

This was probably a fool's errand. Carson had likely already checked the treehouse. If he knew about it.

Finally the tree she'd been seeking came into view. She

stood at the base, trying to see if Mark was on the platform, but it was impossible to tell.

"Mark, are you there? It's me, Vi—Lily."

There was rustling, then silence again. Finally a voice called down to her. "Is the pastor with you?"

Exhaling in relief, she answered quickly, "No, I'm alone."

No response.

"Can I talk to you?"

"I guess." There was a distinct lack of enthusiasm to his tone.

"Would you come down? I can't climb up there one-handed, and I really don't want to keep yelling."

Another long pause, then she heard rustling movements. A moment later Mark slid his legs over the treehouse platform and started down. He had a large piece of fabric on his back, twisted like a sling. Had he gone so far as to pack his belongings before he left? Then she looked closer as he made his descent. Was the sling moving?

Mark jumped down the last few feet and turned to face her. "What did you want to talk about?"

Before she could answer, she heard whimpering coming from the sling on his back. So there *was* some kind of critter in there. "Do you want to introduce me to your friend first?"

His brow furrowed as he met her gaze with a wary look. For a moment she thought he would refuse. But he finally nodded and slipped out of the sling. He placed the bundle on the grass, and immediately the head of a dog popped up. Mark scooped the animal up and held it protectively, as if he expected her to try to take it from him.

Violet studied the pooch, finding it to be a small, beagle-looking mutt with oversized ears and paws that looked too big for his body.

"Who is this?" She slowly extended her hand so the animal could sniff it.

"Rocky."

"Hello, Rocky." The dog's tail gave a little wag, so she moved her hand to scratch his head. "Is he yours?"

Mark shifted. "I'm taking care of him."

"Oh?"

"His back paw don't work right. See? And he didn't have anyone else."

"I see." And she did. Mark no doubt saw the dog's lack of a place to belong as a mirror of his own situation. "So, how did you come up with the name Rocky?"

"I named him after my momma." He kept his focus on the dog. "Her name was Rebecca Olivia Kemp. She used to tell me her initials spelled out ROK because she was my rock and I'd always be able to count on her." He looked up then, his eyes suspiciously moist. "I miss her so much."

"I know. And you probably will for a very long time. But you have other people in your life you can count on. Like me. And like Pastor Carson."

He stiffened and his lips tightened. But he didn't say anything.

"Pastor Carson is looking for you," she said softly. "He's very worried."

"I don't believe you."

So this had something to do with Carson. "Why would you say such a thing?"

Mark kicked at the ground. "He only took me in in the first place because he feels guilty."

"Oh, Mark, I'm sure that's not true."

Mark looked up at her with anguished eyes. "But it is. He feels guilty because he's responsible for my father's death."

She couldn't control the gasp that escaped her throat. Surely the boy had it wrong. "Did someone tell you this?"

"My momma wrote him a letter about it. I found it today." He met her gaze with earnest intensity. "I wasn't snooping, I promise. I went in his study to get a new pencil when mine broke, and I accidentally knocked over his Bible. When I was picking it up, the letter fell out and I could tell it was my momma's handwriting. And I just had to read what she wrote to him."

Violet's mind was whirling, trying to figure out how to handle this in the best way possible for this hurting boy. "And she accused the pastor of killing your father." Was the boy's mother a liar?

"Not directly. But it was all his fault. He won my father's total life savings in a poker game. That's why my dad went home and killed himself."

His gambling. She placed a hand on the boy's shoulder. "Mark, I'm so sorry that happened to you and your mother. It's always a terrible thing when a loved one takes their own life." She gave his shoulder a squeeze. "But surely you can understand that Pastor Carson never forced your father to play in that poker game or to wager all of his money."

Mark just shrugged. Then he met her gaze. "But he kept it from me. It looks to me like he felt plenty guilty."

"Your mother kept it from you too," she said gently. "The pastor was probably just waiting until you were a little bit older."

The boy shifted but didn't say anything.

"Even if the pastor first took you in out of a sense of guilt or obligation, he really does care about you now. Don't doubt that. I can see it in the way he acts when he's around you, how he feels protective and proud and how genuinely worried he was when he came around looking for you earlier." She straightened. "Now don't you think you've made him suffer enough? Let's get you back home and the two of you can talk."

He nodded, then paused. "He doesn't know about Rocky yet."

She grinned. "Now might be an excellent time to tell him.

But I can take Rocky home with me until you two work things out." Then she straightened and offered him a bracing smile. "It'll all work out okay, you'll see."

Mark didn't look convinced, but he tightened his hold on the dog and nodded.

As they marched side by side across the field, Violet prayed she could track Carson down quickly.

17

He was a self-righteous pharisee, a hypocrite who had pointed to the splinter in her eye while being blind to the plank in his own. Carson paced back and forth across his study. Violet had not only brought Mark home safe and sound yesterday evening, but she'd somehow convinced Mark to hear him out.

He and Mark had had a very long, very emotional talk and had finally reached a point where Carson thought they'd be able to move forward and build a true relationship, if not father-son, then perhaps more like uncle-nephew. And he owed it in large part to Violet. During his talk with Mark, the boy had relayed the conversation he'd had with her.

He checked the clock on his bookcase. The dress shop would be opening soon. Time for him to do a bit of groveling.

As soon as Violet spotted him walking in the door, he saw her brace herself as if ready for a blow. And he mentally called himself every kind of cad all over again.

He paused, leaving some distance between them. "Can we talk?" he asked as humbly as he could manage.

She titled her chin up, and he was glad to see her spunk was back. "Of course. If you'll actually let me talk this time."

Carson winced. "I deserved that. And yes, I promise."

He opened the shop door, and she preceded him onto the sidewalk. He directed their steps toward the schoolhouse road. It was relatively quiet there this time of year, and he didn't want to be disturbed by passersby until he said what he'd come to say. They strolled in silence for a little while, but the tension of unsaid things practically hummed between them.

"How's Mark this morning?" she finally asked.

"He's well. I don't think he'll be running away again, at least not over this."

"So he's content with your explanations."

"Let's just say he's willing to discuss it in terms of how everyone makes mistakes and how we can't always see how our actions can hurt others. I'm sure we'll have many more discussions on the matter, but it helps that I had other letters from his mother besides the one he read so he could see how she viewed the situation."

"That's good. The two of you belong together; you're good for each other. I'd hate to see something like this break you apart."

Which was his opening. "About the way I verbally attack—"

She held up a hand, halting his words. "You promised to listen to what I had to say first."

He clamped his lips closed and nodded.

"I want you to know I do understand that what I did was wrong and I regret it deeply, at least the part where I deceived everyone. I don't regret the time I got to spend here and the people I met."

"I'm glad for that as well."

"Please. I'm not finished." She kept her gaze focused straight ahead. "I also want you to know that I talked Lily into this, not the other way around. You shouldn't hold any of this against her when she returns." Again she tilted her chin up. "As for where she will be returning from, while I've been living her life here, she's been living my life." Violet cut him a quick sideways glance. "I'm not the woman you think I am. My life is nothing like Lily's. For the past six years, my best friend and I have been performers in a traveling show. Wyatt has a trick riding act, and I have a sharpshooter act."

Well, that certainly explained a few things. "So when I found you doing target practice, that wasn't some casual hobby."

She shook her head. "The thing is, I perform my act wearing a costume and I'm known as the Masked Marvel. My identity is supposed to remain a secret to give my character an added air of mystery. So when I hurt my wrist, it put that in jeopardy. If the Masked Marvel and plain old Violet Taylor were both walking around in slings, it wouldn't take much to put two and two together."

"I see. That's why you had Lily take your place. But I find it hard to picture your sister firing a pistol, much less doing it with any degree of accuracy."

That teased a grin from Violet. "She hasn't had to. The Masked Marvel is appearing wearing the mask and sling and not shooting at all. Instead, she's just mingling with the crowd, signing autographs and such. Then 'Violet' is mingling without the sling so no one suspects anything."

"That's why you showed up with the sling and planned to leave when it comes off."

She nodded. "And I didn't mean to fall— I mean I didn't intend to mess everything up."

He hoped her little verbal slip meant what he thought it did. They'd reached the schoolyard by then but kept walking on past it. Before long the road had narrowed and was

155

bordered by woods and open fields. "Tell me, do you enjoy the circus life?"

She shrugged. "It's been very good to me. When I was sixteen, my grandfather died and I didn't have any money or any way to earn a living. Then Wyatt heard about the circus and concocted this idea that we could come up with an act of our own and try to convince the circus to give us a chance."

"Who is this Wyatt you keep speaking of?" He couldn't quite extinguish a little flicker of jealousy—she said the name with such affection.

"His mother was the cook on my grandfather's ranch, and the two of us practically grew up together. He's like an over-protective big brother."

Feeling a little better, he tried again. "I got us off track. You never answered my question. Do you enjoy the circus life? If you had a choice, and finances weren't an issue, would you want to continue?"

"No, not anymore."

The hope he was trying to hold at bay flared up. "Violet, I know I was wrong in the way I confronted you over this deception. The fact that I was almost immediately forced to face my own lie of omission made it abundantly clear that I live in a very fragile glass house. Can you forgive me?"

She offered him a shy smile. "It is already done."

He helped her sit on a large boulder half-buried near the side of the road. "That's a relief to hear. Because, Violet Taylor, I love you, and if you'd let me, I'd like to court you properly in the hopes of winning you over."

VIOLET'S HEART nearly turned over in her chest. It was the words she longed to hear. Then she paused to search his face. "Are you sure? You don't really know me after all. Up until three days ago you thought I was Lily. And I'm *not* Lily. I know nothing about fashion and feminine fripperies, I don't light up a room the way she does, and I can't be bubbly even if I tried. I'm Violet, that rather odd girl who shoots better than most men, who spent the past six years living a very unconventional life as a performer in a traveling show, who before she came here had no idea how to settle down and live the life of a townie."

"You're wrong—I do know you. In fact, even before I knew your name, somewhere deep inside I knew you weren't Lily. I know your heart and your courage and your generous spirit. Those are the things that matter, that make you uniquely you. And those things are quite beautiful to me."

He leaned down and stroked her cheek, not worried about who might see. "I don't expect you to feel the same. That's why I said I'd like to court you. I hope to give you time to decide if perhaps you can develop feelings for me."

She smiled and returned his gesture, stroking his cheek with the back of her hand. "Oh Carson, don't you understand? When I said I don't want to go back to the circus life, it's because I would like to build a life here with you. I love your earnest concern for people, your strength of character, and your courage in facing your own frailties. And I just plain love *you*."

And with that he pulled her into an embrace and gave her the kiss she'd been longing for ever since that Sunday afternoon in the storeroom.

Epilogue

I am *Mrs. Carson Davis. I am Mrs. Carson Davis. I* am *Mrs. Carson Davis.*

Violet sat at the vanity in the bedroom she now shared with Carson and looked at herself in the mirror. Of all the identities she'd assumed over the years—Violet Mayfield, Violet Taylor, the Masked Marvel, Lily Mayfield—this was her favorite. And as of one week ago it had become officially hers.

She glanced down at the mahogany box, which sat on a corner of the dressing table. Violet smiled as she opened the lid and ran a finger across the pistol's pink mother-of-pearl handle. Truth to tell, she was still skeptical of the pistol's matchmaking properties, but she was willing to concede that the accompanying advice to open her heart to love had played a part in her current happiness. And for that she'd be forever grateful to Kitty Horwath Easton. Hers was the last name on the series of notes accompanying the pistol, so Violet assumed she was the one who'd handed it off to her.

She pulled the note from its special pocket in the lining and read over the contents one last time. She felt a sisterhood to the other five women who'd inscribed their own happily-ever-afters there, five women she'd never met but who shared more than a temporary ownership of the pink pistol. Because they, too, had each found a man who was steadfast and true, a man moreover whom she could both cherish and be cherished by.

It was time.

Without hesitation she added her own testament to the bottom of the note.

Sharpshooter Violet Taylor married Pastor Carson Davis on July 1, 1911. Keeping secrets threatened to ruin our shot at love. But when we found the courage to come clean to each other, the smoke cleared and we were able to joyfully embrace what promises to be a bright future together.

Before she could refold the note, she heard footsteps coming up the stairs.

"Hello there, Mrs. Davis," a familiar voice said with a grin in his voice. She looked up in time to see him in the mirror as he leaned down to wrap his arm around her.

"Hello there, Mr. Davis," she replied, leaning back into his embrace.

"I have good news."

"Do you now."

Carson released her momentarily to help her stand and face him. Then he pulled her into a more comfortable embrace. "This morning I set the wheels in motion for us to formally adopt Mark."

"Oh, Carson, that's wonderful." She snuggled against his chest, loving the feel of his arms around her. "I know we're already a family, but it'll be so nice to make it all official."

He planted a kiss on the top of her head. "Were you adding your contribution to the note when I walked in?"

"I was. Would you like to read it?" Determined not to keep any more secrets from the man she loved, Violet had shown Carson the notes that came with the pistol weeks ago.

"I'm too busy at the moment," he said, his breath warm against her ear. "I'll read it later."

Violet smiled, that now-familiar warmth emanating from her chest and flooding her body. She wrapped her arms around Carson's neck, reveling in the fact that he welcomed such intimacies from her.

His hand came up to brush her cheek, his touch gentle, his hold possessive, his gaze achingly tender. "I hope you know, I thank God every day for bringing you into my life."

"As do I," Violet responded, lifting her face for his kiss. "As do I."

THE END

If you enjoyed Violet and Carson's story, a review on Amazon would be much appreciated.

ONE SHOT AT LOVE

By Linda Broday

Panther Creek, Colorado
1939

The tall pines surrounding Panther Creek, Colorado stood silent, weeping for what once was. The summer of 1939 began slowly in no rush to go anywhere. Once a thriving community, it was now home to the defunct Gunbarrel Mine. Ghosts and a few hardy souls continued to call it home because they had nowhere left to go.

Mariah Bartee sighed and stared out the window of the small general store where she worked, sadness gripping her heart. She still missed her parents who'd both flown home to Glory, leaving her to raise her younger brother and sister.

Her father perished three years ago in a bad mining explosion. Her mother followed a year later after a horrible fall from a cliff during a blinding snowstorm. Gone. Just like that.

On the mountain, death could come in an instant. Life seemed fragile at best.

She glanced toward her shotgun propped beside the door. Rough men inhabited these steep trails and danger lurked, both from the two-legged as well as the four-legged animals.

It paid to keep her wits about her.

The train whistle blew as it came to the small station. Mariah wondered how many hobos would get off and cook themselves a meal before getting back on. They were harmless and her brother Robby and little sister Sweet Sue dearly loved to sit with the hobos around their fire, listening to their stories. Some folks might disapprove but the kids could do far worse.

At the very least, they'd see what not to become and maybe the lessons in life would do them good. The Depression that started in 1929 didn't affect mountain people like them too much seeing as how they were poor to start with. But she heard people in the cities had it bad and some had committed suicide according to newspaper accounts. For the most part, Mariah and her siblings had already learned to do without.

Mr. Freeman, the owner of the store, came to stand beside her, his thumbs in his suspenders. "The train's on time."

"I wonder what it would be like to climb aboard and ride away with no destination in mind." In fact, Mariah daydreamed about going to the city just to see different scenery. "I hear they have moving picture shows and dance halls."

"Pshaw!" Freeman blew out a breath and scratched his bald head. "I took the wife to Boulder, and we couldn't wait to get back to the mountain. The noise about drove us batty and people honked their horns at us all the time for holding up traffic. Then our Model A died in an intersection and everyone yelled their lungs out, threatening to shoot us. I told the missus it would be a long time before I went back. If ever."

The Freemans owned one of the few automobiles and to Mariah that made him rich. She was fine riding a horse or a mule. Vehicles were always breaking down, getting flat tires, or running out of gas. They didn't seem very dependable.

She was about to turn away and finish dusting the shelves when an old Model T, trailing smoke, pulled up in front of the store, coughing and sputtering.

Mr. Freeman chuckled. "That tin lizzy's seen better days."

"I wonder who he is." Mariah took in the young man's brown vest and fedora. He climbed out and kicked a tire. "Whoever he is, he's not happy."

His white shirt sleeves rolled to the elbows, the stranger strode into the store. His smile looked a little forced. "Howdy, can I trouble you for some water? My motor needs cooling."

"Of course. There's a hydrant outside. Help yourself." Freeman shook his hand. "We don't often get visitors through Panther Creek so you'll have to excuse us for staring. I'm Joe Freeman, the owner of this store. And Mariah here runs it."

The stranger passed a curious gaze at Mariah and nodded, taking Freeman's offered hand. "Dax Talon." He scanned the shelves. "Nice place you have here."

"Thank you. It suits our needs and serves the few remaining people here. Most moved away when the mine shut down, but we have about a hundred or so stubborn hangers-on." Freeman dropped Talon's hand and glanced out at the car. "Your lizzy ain't faring so well in the high altitudes of the mountains."

"No, sir. She runs well down below and I can't complain but here I might as well have a horse." Talon turned to Mariah. "I'm looking for someone—my sister. A young lady about your age. I heard I might find her around here. I've been searching for Rosanna ever since she was taken a year ago on her seventeenth birthday."

Freeman scratched his head in thought. "Rosanna. Rosanna. What does she look like?"

"She's slender, not as tall as your helper, and has reddish-brown hair. Her disappearance has left our parents in poor health, so it's fallen to me to find her. I promised my father."

"What makes you think she's here on our mountain?" Mariah asked quietly.

"Ma'am, I've pretty much followed the path the abductors took to Denver. There it went cold." He paused and glanced out the window. "Then I recently got a letter from a man saying I should look for Levy Tyler in Panther Creek so here I am."

The name Levy Tyler sent chills over Mariah. The man scared her with his violent ways. Everyone on the mountain with half sense steered clear of the Tylers.

"I don't know what you've heard, Mr. Talon, but…I hope you brought a gun." Mariah hated the hardness of her tone, but Talon needed to be aware of the danger.

Freeman scoffed. "Now, Mariah, don't go scaring him."

"Just laying out the facts. The Tylers are moonshiners, and they shoot anyone who comes near their still. Folks around here don't bother them. If Levy took your sister, she's not had it easy." Mariah pitied Dax Talon. She truly did. Even if he got his sister back, she'd never be the same. "I recall a girl with Levy quite a while back. She looked scared. Never heard her name spoken so I don't know if she was your sister."

The young girl's sunken eyes and pale face had haunted her for days. Mariah's gut had told her something wasn't right. But they had no law to turn to in Panther Creek.

"When exactly did she disappear?" Freeman asked, rocking back on his heels.

"September 15th. That was Rosanna's birthday." Talon swallowed hard. "Thank you, Miss Mariah. This gives me something to go on." He looked away. "This has taken a heavy toll on our family." He ducked his head as though he'd said too much and stepped toward the screen door.

She patted the sides of her hair that she'd pulled back and

tied with a string then instantly dropped her hands. She didn't trust men, especially ones with pretty faces.

Yet Talon seemed different. It was the sincerity in his eyes. A man could lie about everything but his eyes always gave him away.

She lowered her lashes and studied him through the dark fringe. What she could see of his hair under his hat appeared to be the color of freshly plowed earth. His sleeves rolled to his elbows revealed thick veins along his muscular arms. Lean waist, broad shoulders.

Nice.

For some reason, Mariah felt compelled to add, "Good luck in your search."

He swung around with a smile and tipped his hat. "Thank you, ma'am. It was nice meeting you and Mr. Freeman. I'll be around until I find what I came after. If you think of something, I've rented a room at Miss Nancy's."

The door shut behind him. He raised the hood, strode to the hydrant where a hose was attached, and proceeded to cool his radiator.

"What do you think of him?" Mariah asked.

"He's a nice young man and his mother taught him manners." Freeman released a loud breath. "If Levy Tyler, or any of the Tylers, has his sister, I feel sorry for her. She won't be the same person he once knew."

"It's sad." She brightened. "Maybe she's not with the Tylers. Please, for her sake. I want to help Talon find her."

"Mariah, watch out and don't let your guard down."

"For goodness sakes, Mr. Freeman, I'm not crazy." She went back to dusting the shelves but couldn't help glancing out the window once in a while.

When Talon finally finished and drove off, an odd feeling of loss came over her. Shrugging, she tackled the back room and unpacked a box of pickles, forgetting all about the handsome stranger who'd come to their mountain. He wasn't for her.

No one had his sights set on Mariah and that's just the way it was.

Of the men in the area, there were none she'd consider marrying for even a moment. They thought her uppity, but she knew how she wanted to be treated and if she couldn't get that, she'd stay an old maid.

It was a few minutes to five when the screen door slammed and she heard her brother Robby yelling, "Mariah! Where are you, Mariah?"

Her heart pounding, she stepped from the storeroom. "What is it?"

Her nine-year-old sister, Sweet Sue, burst out, "Come quick! We found some bones!"

Books in the Pink Pistol Sisterhood Series

In Her Sights by **Karen Witemeyer**
Book 1 ~ March 30
Love on Target **by Shanna Hatfield**
Book 2 ~ April 10
Love Under Fire **by Cheryl Pierson**
Book 3 ~ April 20
Bulletproof Bride **by Kit Morgan**
Book 4 ~ April 30
Bullseye Bride **by Kari Trumbo**
Book 5 ~ May 10
Disarming His Heart **by Winnie Griggs**
Book 6 ~ May 20
One Shot at Love **by Linda Broday**
Book 7 ~ May 30
Armed & Marvelous **by Pam Crooks**
Book 8 ~ June 10
Lucky Shot **by Shanna Hatfield**
Book 9 ~ June 20
Aiming for His Heart **by Julie Benson**
Book 10 ~ June 30
Pistol Perfect **by Jessie Gussman**
Book 11 ~ July 10

See all the Pink Pistol Sisterhood Books at
www.petticoatsandpistols.com.

ABOUT WINNIE

Winnie Griggs has written over 30 works of historical and Amish romance. Her stories are always emotional and heart-warming and live up to her promise to always deliver tales of Small Towns, Big Hearts, Amazing Grace.

She's won numerous writing awards, among them a prestigious RT Reviewers' Choice Award, and she's also hit the Publishers' Weekly Bestseller List for Religious Fiction.

Winnie lives with her own romance hero, a rancher whose white steed looks a whole lot like a large tractor, and together they're building their own happily-ever-after.

Winnie loves to hear from readers. Her email is winnie@winniegriggs.com.

You can keep up on the latest news and be entered in her monthly giveaways by subscribing to her newsletter

Other ways to connect with Winnie online:

Website https://www.winniegriggs.com

f facebook.com/WinnieGriggs.Author

BB bookbub.com/authors/winnie-griggs

Made in the USA
Columbia, SC
29 November 2024

47950780R00105